Other Books by Tony Jordan

The Train
Flying Blind
Follow Me and Other Stories
Breakfast with Faulkner

All are available online at Amazon, Barnes and Noble,
Books-a-Million, and Kindle.

SPIES, ASSASSINS, AND SUCH

Tony Jordan

Robin
Look over your shoulder!,
Tony Jordan

SPY HILL
PUBLISHING

Spy Hill Publishing

First Edition

The text of these stories has been approved by the CIA Publications Review
Board.

Library of Congress Control Number: 2017908787
Spy Hill Publishing, Clinton, TN

ISBN-13: 9780692859124
ISBN-10: 0692859128

Book and cover design by Nathan Armistead
Printed in the United States of America

To Miss Anne
My colleague in spying and conspiracy, my friend, my lover
and to my father
who taught me how to charm people by playing the role they
expect of you

(Oops—first secret exposed!)

Acknowledgments

To ALL THE SPIES, SOURCES, agents, assets—and especially to the spymasters, counterspies, and all the really bad people—who unknowingly helped me write these stories, my many thanks.

Contents

Preface

THESE STORIES ARE THE MUSINGS of an old spymaster sitting on his porch sipping a really good, twenty-four-year-old single malt. Lord knows I never thought I would get here. To paraphrase Peter Falk in the 1979 movie *The In-Laws*, "The CIA has a really excellent retirement program. The secret is staying alive long enough to collect it."

Enjoy!

SPIES, ASSASSINS, AND SUCH

(OH MY!)

"Eyes"

January 19——, Arab Africa

He pulled the cotton wrap around his shoulders and head, like an old woman's shawl. Thin, it gave him only minor protection from the morning chill. Later, the heat would come, and the cloth would shade him against the strong burn of the African sun. One hand held the wrap in place while he lifted the other in supplication to the drivers stopping for the traffic light. The morning traffic was heavy, but he had only twenty dinars in the drawstring purse tied to his waist.

This was a very good spot because it was the single road that funneled traffic from the section of the city where most foreigners lived. It came around the airport from the north and narrowed as it passed under the railroad bridge, where there was a traffic light. The road passing the airport to the south had no such natural stopping point, and the drivers were too busy attempting to merge their cars into the already-heavy flow of traffic on Airport Road to pay attention to those who beseeched in the name of Allah.

A few of the drivers who stopped for the light would throw a coin, and sometimes, if a foreigner was the lead car in the line, he would receive an entire pound...one hundred dinars! When that occurred he truly thanked Allah; otherwise, he was too busy trying to pull himself out of the way of trucks and avoid breathing the diesel exhaust fumes that flowed from the tailpipes of many of the vehicles. A good thing his face was already black, for were it not, it would be at the end of any day at the intersection.

The traffic stayed at a good volume all through the day, but other, more mobile, beggars came for the rushes just after second prayers, at lunchtime, and just before the afternoon prayers. They moved from car to car while he remained anchored at the corner, his hands raised like those of all beggars. For that is what he was, a beggar. But in begging, he realized the opportunity to help others. For giving alms was one of the pillars of Islam, and in offering himself to the religious, he gave them the chance to earn favor with Allah. There was, then, nothing mean in what he did. He felt himself an agent of Allah, chosen to assist others in achieving heaven and to feel good about themselves in this world. Surely Allah would remember him in the next world, and he would not have to crawl through heaven on crippled legs.

At dark, he would drag himself back to the shed he shared with five others, hoping not to be accosted by the teenagers who often stole his money. For if Allah was kind in sending the religious to him during the day, that same Allah seemed unable to see in the darkness, when the ungodly took to the streets. Could Allah not, just once, smite them with a lightning bolt?

Perhaps he could afflict them with pox, or some other disease. Once, in a dream, the beggar wished Allah would burden them with polio, but he quickly recanted and asked Allah's forgiveness because none should be so afflicted. The pain was great and the consequences unbearable. Still, he did bear it.

Today, the heat did not come. It remained cloudy, and there was a heavy wetness to the air. The smoke hung more closely to the ground. The windows were up in the cars, the drivers busy trying to keep their windshields clean. The smoke and pollution mixed with the wet to form an oil-like film on their windows. Many of the older cars did not have wipers that worked, and the drivers hurriedly left their vehicles to wipe their windshields with already-dirty cloths as they stopped for the light. They were too busy to notice him there on the corner, his hands in the air, his voice entreating them to give for the love of Allah. Tonight, the ruffians would achieve little if they took the purse from his waist.

He had, some time ago, taken to carrying a second, smaller pouch inside his thobe. He had stuffed it with cloth and when he needed to relieve himself he would crawl to the ditch. He would remove the larger-value coins, and any paper pounds he had received, and place them in the bag, which he stuffed back between his legs to look as though it was his penis. The stuffing kept the coins from jingling. Thus, those who would rob beggars received only enough to keep them from hurting him in anger. It was a toll he must pay. They taunted him that he could do no better, but they had yet to guess he had more. They were not among Allah's wisest creatures, and he hoped they would remain that way.

It was winter. The desert could be very cold after dark any day but especially so in winter. Today was not good for alms, and he was cold and wet, so he began the tiring trip to his shed early. Alas, it was not early enough, for as he approached the last corner before his sanctuary, there, in the failing light, waited the four youths. They wore jackets over their Western clothes, and they had shoes. If they could afford such luxuries, why did they need his meager income?

The largest of the four approached him. "Salaam alaikum, Salah. Do you have alms for the poor today?"

"Oh, Ali! Today was not good. The cold, the wet. I have but a few dinars, and I need them for food. In the name of Allah, do not take what little I have."

"But, Salah, all men must give alms. It is the rule of Allah. Do you believe yourself better than others? Do you yourself not need to give alms to the needy? My friends and I, we are needy. We need cigarettes and hashish. Would you deny us what little pleasures are left to us?" He laughed as he bent to snatch the purse from Salah's waist. It did not come easily, and in the pulling, Salah was thrown on his side, his thobe opening as he fell.

"What is this?" the smallest of the four said as he reached between Salah's legs.

"A second purse! Look! Look! It is filled with money. We are rich!" He danced as he pulled a bill from the sock and emptied the coins on the ground. Salah scrambled to pull himself upright and grabbed to recover the coins as they fell.

Ali grabbed his wrist, forcing his hand open and taking the coins. "Holding back on us. That is not smart, crippled one. Perhaps you need a reminder of your place in the world."

"And where would that place be?" a tenor voice asked in Koranic Arabic.

The light had continued to fail, but turning his head, Salah saw a man of medium height in a white thobe, his head covered with the long white ghutra of a sheik. He had dark hair and a moustache, and his skin—while brown—seemed somehow lighter. He stood behind the four who quickly turned to face him. The man addressed himself to Ali. His voice was the voice of someone accustomed to command and someone who expected to be obeyed.

"Return his money and leave," he said slowly.

Ali, as tall as the stranger and somewhat bulkier, drew himself up. "This is no business of yours, stranger. You need to leave before we teach you your place as well." He stepped toward the stranger menacingly, and the other three closed a step as well.

Ali did not observe the minute changes to the stranger's posture as the man shifted his weight to the balls of his feet, his knees bending ever so slightly. The stranger's left arm came up to his waist; his right hung straight at his side.

"Ali, is it? Then, Ali, let me explain that indeed I know my place and do not need you to guide me in that manner. But perhaps a lesson for you and your friends is in order."

Ali's lunge did not quite reach the stranger, for from out of the man's right hand appeared a rod with which he struck Ali, first in the ribs, and then between his shoulder and his neck. Ali dropped as if struck by lightning. At the same moment, the stranger lashed his left arm up and out at the elbow, his fist striking a second youth in the face. It happened so fast that Salah could not later relate exactly what happened—other than the second youth fell as a sack of wheat from the back of a truck. Spinning on his toes, the stranger jabbed the rod into the third youth's stomach causing him to fall to his knees and double over. The fourth youth he grabbed by his jacket front.

"You will pick up all the money and put it back in the purse," the stranger said, his voice steady and controlled.

The fourth youth, Samir by name, did as he was instructed. It took him several minutes, during which the stranger addressed Salah.

"Are you hurt? Do you need to see a doctor?"

Salah had no concept of seeing a doctor for he had never seen or been seen by a doctor in his life.

"No, I am hurt no more than ever. I can go on, but I fear tomorrow I will be hurt, for these are not children of Allah, but followers of Shaitan. Still, I thank you. May Allah bless and protect you for your actions."

The stranger stepped aside and bent down, striking the ground with his rod. It disappeared into his hand.

"Truly, this is no man," Salah thought, "but a magician who can command a weapon from the air." Samir's wide eyes betrayed that he was as amazed as Salah. Ali, unable to speak, but able to see, had watched as the weapon disappeared into the stranger's hand as well.

The stranger stood over Ali as Samir handed Salah the sock with the money—or as much of it as he could find—stuffed back into its heel and toe. Stepping on Ali's wrist—which opened his closed fist—the stranger reached down and removed the coins Ali had taken from Salah. He handed them to Salah, who put both hands out as if in supplication. The thought struck Salah that this action seemed somehow familiar. It was as if he experienced an episode of déjà vu.

The stranger instructed Samir to help Ali stand. As he did so, the stranger approached and, standing close to the two, said quietly, "Salah now enjoys the protection of the Brotherhood, as do those who reside with him. Disturb his life, take his money, or in any other manner interfere with him, and you will feel not just the wrath of Allah but that of the Brotherhood. In fact, I shall have people checking, and I no longer want to see you in this neighborhood. Fail to follow these instructions, and your families will recover your bodies from the Nile, that is, unless the Brothers decide to bury you with a pig's carcass. Now leave."

As the youths staggered into the night, the stranger turned once again to Salah and asked, "Salah can you read and write?" It seemed a strange request of someone in this situation.

"Effendi, I know my letters and numbers, but I have little schooling. While I can write, it is with difficulty because of the calluses on my palms and fingers from dragging my worthless legs through the streets."

"Can your friends read numbers and letters, as well?"

"Oh yes, Effendi. In fact, Mustafah was going to the university before he fell off the bus and lost his legs. He is very well educated, but now he is a beggar like the rest of us, for his family can no longer care for him."

"Tomorrow night I shall return to ensure your tormentors are not as stupid as they look. We shall speak again." The stranger turned to depart.

"Wait, Effendi," Salah asked. "The weapon from your hand, what manner of magic is that? Are you a mage?"

The stranger did not stop, but turning his head slightly said, "I have been called by many names. 'Mage' will do."

Salah, none the worse from his encounter, continued to the shed where Abdul and Mustafah waited. Their day had been no more successful than his, so to hear that the thieves had been routed helped warm them more than the three pieces of charcoal they had been able to afford. When Fahd, Fuad, and Hassan arrived, Salah had to tell the story again. And each time he told it, the mage's right hand struck more like lightning than before, the weapon appearing and disappearing at will.

Each speculated on how Salah had become protected by the Brotherhood, for everyone knew the Brotherhood had been publicly banned even though some members of the government—including the president—were members. But speaking of the Brotherhood was prohibited, so each dropped his voice to a whisper when using its name. They questioned Salah on what he had been doing and to whom he had been talking, but none could fathom why such a thing might happen.

It was Mustafah who questioned why the mage might be interested in whether they could read and write, for such had been lost in the story—overshadowed by the tale of Salah's protection by the Brotherhood. They fell asleep without an answer.

Awakening before the sun, Salah set out for the intersection and, as usual, reached it before the morning rush. Taking up his position, he drew his shawl close and began his supplication in the name of Allah. He remembered his dreams from the night wherein the identity of the mage was just beyond his reach. Throughout the dream he had reached out, and, just as he was about to grasp the memory of where he had seen the mage before, the knowledge had evaporated like the morning mist under the African sun.

Should the mage come, he would ask…or would he? Perhaps it was better not to know. Still, he wondered if what happened had itself been a dream and the mage was simply an image conjured in his imagination.

A Land Cruiser stopped with its window down and, leaning out, a head and arm appeared. No one spoke, but the arm handed a pound note to Salah who accepted it, head bowed. But he looked up as the window was raised and was startled to see what he thought was the face of the mage. "But it could not be," he thought, "for this face, while tan, was foreign. There was no moustache, and the eyes were green. Surely the mage had dark eyes and there was no mistaking his military-style moustache."

"No," he thought, "I have seen the face in my dreams, and now I'm seeing the face wherever I look. I must ask Mustafah why this is so."

True to his word, the mage returned that night and for several more, speaking only to Salah as he made his way home on the darkened street. The first night the mage produced a bag of charcoal. A welcome gift, for it was very cold. The second, a plastic bag with bread and a container of hummus. The third, a carton of cigarettes, from which the friends shared one pack and sold the others, bringing in as many pounds as they could have begged in several days. On each occasion the mage asked Salah about himself and his friends. Where were their families? Was anyone married? Could they operate an invalid tricycle? Did they feel strongly about politics? How well did they know the city…and other such unimportant questions. Salah did not mind the questions, for he was happy that the robbers seemed to have disappeared—at least for the present. Then, on the fifth night, the mage did not come. Nor on the sixth. Salah was disappointed and even stopped for a while near where the mage had spoken to him, hoping that perhaps it was just that the mage had been delayed.

Then, on the seventh night, the mage appeared. He spoke to Salah of a chance to change his life, and that of his friends.

Salah had excitedly delivered the proposal to his friends around a very warm brazier filled with charcoal courtesy of the mage. It was work. Work that cripples could do. No one ever spoke to cripples of work, but here it was. They simply had to watch a house or building and note the visitors. They could keep whatever they begged on the corner of the street, and in addition, the mage would pay them five pounds a day, each!

"But why?" Mustafah asked. "Why does he want us to watch?"

"Is it important?" Salah countered. "Perhaps it is for the Brotherhood. It is work, and I say we accept it."

The others agreed. Even Mustafah could offer no objection to the thought of twenty-five pounds a day income.

Then, at the beginning of the third week, on returning from his long trip dragging himself across too many streets,

Salah found, parked outside the shed, an invalid tricycle that could carry two people. One drove and operated the arm-driven sprocket, and the other rode on the seat next to him. After that, the friends took turns dropping one another off at the corners appointed them by the mage. In the eighth week, a bag appeared on the seat of the tricycle. It contained five cartons of cigarettes with a note from the mage.

"Instead of begging on Sharia Abdulaziz, sell these cigarettes. You may keep the money you make, but watch closely number fourteen for foreigners. Burn this note with tonight's charcoal."

In the twelfth week, a case of colas was added to the cigarettes, and in the twentieth, cigarette lighters and some candies. The money they made from selling these items enabled the five to move from the shed to a former garage that actually had a charcoal stove and a concrete floor. They agreed to use some of the money they made to buy other products, which they sold for slight markups. But still, they watched, and on occasion the mage provided them what he called "bonuses" for their good work.

They did not stop begging, for that allowed them to go wherever they pleased. It was not acceptable to chase away a beggar. And even if they received little in the way of alms, the mage paid them for what they saw.

Although he still spoke with Salah mostly, the mage had taken to speaking also with Mustafah. On one occasion he gave Mustafah a great deal of money and told him to open an account in a local bank. Then he spoke to him in great detail about what had occurred. To whom had he spoken? What was the physical detail of the office? Was there another office in the back of the space? Did he see a man who looked like…?

Mustafah answered all the questions well. At the end of the conversation, the mage smiled and thanked Mustafah for his work. As the mage rose to leave, Mustafah asked what he should do about the money he had put in the bank.

"Oh," said the mage, "that belongs to the five of you. Consider it a bonus."

When Mustafah related this to the others, Fuad could barely control himself. He kept remarking, "It is like magic! We are beggars, but we have a bank account. We live in a room with a concrete floor. We have a tricycle and can go anywhere in the city we want. We have the protection of the Brotherhood. It is magic!"

"It is like magic," Salah thought as he sat at the intersection the next day. He was begging, but he was looking for two specific cars. He was to note the time they came through the intersection, the number and description of the people in the cars and the direction they took from the intersection. Since they were unique cars, they would not be too difficult to find. He had done this before. The day before he had looked for the same cars at a different intersection. He did not know how the mage knew where to look, but when he asked Salah to look, the cars or people for whom he looked were invariably there.

As he invoked others in the name of Allah, a Land Cruiser stopped, the window down, and as before, a head and arm appeared. The hand held a pound for him. He received it and once again experienced déjà vu. The mage has a foreigner who looks like him. He would tell the mage tonight. It would amuse him.

The Land Cruiser continued straight through the intersection, past the university, and toward the center of town. Just past the parliament, it turned down Sharia Latif and into the parking lot of the American embassy.

A man in his forties, of medium height, emerged. He wore khaki pants, a long-sleeved khaki shirt, and a photographer's vest. His head was shaded by a Panama straw hat, and he carried a small leather briefcase. He showed a badge to the local guard and entered the embassy. He took the elevator to one of the upper floors and, after pushing a buzzer, was allowed into a set of rooms that had windows covered with projectile resistant Lexan and a mirrorlike coating that prevented those in buildings across the street from being able to see into the offices. A secretary greeted him and noted, "The chief's finally back, and he wants to see you."

Proceeding to his office at the end of the hallway, he dropped the briefcase on a chair and hung his hat on a hook behind the door where a white thobe and ghutra already hung. He unfastened the ballistic nylon holster from his right forearm and placed it, together with the tempered steel expandable baton it contained, on the front edge of his desk. He took off his vest and pistol belt, dropping them on top of his briefcase, then stepped next door to the chief's office.

"You wanted to see me?"

"You bet! I've been going over your expense account, and I just don't understand some of these things you're buying. An invalid tricycle? Cartons of cigarettes? Twelve dozen sodas? How can all this be operational?"

"What's the total?" the man asked.

"Pretty close to a thousand dollars when you do the conversion from local currency," the chief responded. "How can I explain this to Washington?"

"Well…" the man replied, rubbing his hand across his mouth. "Why don't you start by pointing out the number of intelligence reports we've produced since you've been gone? Mention how we've documented the presence of major international terror organizations in the city. You might add that we're on the verge of proving the host government is not just tolerant of terrorism, but that some senior members are actively supporting international terror groups right here in the city and at their training camps in the desert. Perhaps you could say that by this time next month we'll know the names of individuals in the United States who are not just sympathetic to these organizations, but who are providing both money and materials to help their causes. We'll provide chapter and verse that will enable a legal investigation in the United States, which—I'm sure—will lead to the identification of plans to attack American targets both inside the United States and abroad."

"What?" The chief pushed back from his desk. "You're that close? You'll have proof? Why am I just finding out about this now?"

The man replied, "Well, between your temporary duty in Cairo and your home leave, you've been away from the station for the better part of the past six months. Did you think we stopped work just because you were in Cairo, London, or Rapid City, South Dakota?"

That evening the mage provided Salah, Mustafa, and Fuad with three small nylon travel bags. They looked ragged, and the straps were just barely attached. They could have been something picked out of the garbage at a foreigner's house. But inside each of these tattered, discolored bags was a small camera focused to infinity, the lens anchored behind a small piece of very fine mesh matching the color of the outside of the bag. The mage instructed each of the now-competent operatives on how to set the bags on the ground, point them at a target, and using a remote switch, snap a picture. He then gave each of them specific instructions on where to set up for the next four days. He told them to take pictures of everyone entering or leaving the houses and to note the license plates of any vehicle that brought someone to the house. He also wanted to know if anyone said anything they could overhear.

On the evening of the fourth day, they returned the bags to him, and each provided the information they had obtained. Only Salah had been accosted by anyone during the four days. At one point, a man had emerged from a big black car and had said in very poor Arabic, "You there, cripple, move along!" Salah laughed when he told the story, for the man had immediately been chastised by his companion with the remark, "What kind of Islam do they practice in America? Don't you know that giving alms to the poor is required of us, and if the poor are crippled, our giving is even greater in the eyes of Allah?" Here he had thrown a coin to Salah who had caught it, folded his hands in front of his face, and pronounced, "Shukran, Saeed. Al'hamdulilah." The others laughed when Salah told the story because Salah said he had almost dropped the remote control camera device when he caught the coin but had still managed to take three or four photographs of both the men. Then, with a wry smile, Salah said he hoped Allah would properly instruct the American in the giving of alms.

Developing the film, the mage sorted out the best photographs. Later, using various passport photos and other bits and pieces he had collected over the past several months, he began to compile his analysis of who was doing what, to whom, and for whom.

He crafted a detailed matrix that cataloged meetings between senior host-government officials and known terrorists, and between those same terrorists and American residents who had traveled to the country under the guise of attending religious training courses. The matrix enabled a series of intelligence reports that allowed federal prosecutors and the FBI to obtain necessary warrants for legal efforts to stop planned terrorist activity inside the United States, and it provided crucial documentation that could be shared with friendly governments in Europe and Asia.

The investigations initiated based on the information he provided led to the discovery of three separate conspiracies against American targets. The FBI and several foreign liaison services used the information to orchestrate operations that resulted in the collection of additional evidence linking international terrorist groups with supporters in several third countries. Once all the mechanisms and personnel were identified, quiet diplomatic overtures by the Department of State forced subtle and not-so-subtle changes at high levels.

Privately, members of the Brotherhood came to the conclusion that one of their own had betrayed them. Thus began an internal inquisition leading to charge and countercharge. The hunt for the traitor reached the innermost levels of the Brotherhood, and slowly the organization began to tear itself apart. Members—seeking the safety of numbers—chose sides, and the resulting fragmentation greatly reduced the organization's ability to covertly encourage terrorist groups and to provide resources for anti-American activities in other countries. The Brotherhood might, in the future, recover its footing and once again pose a serious threat, but for the time being, it was rendered impotent as insiders feared possible arrest if they traveled to the United States, Europe, or other key locations.

As with almost all intelligence successes, most of these developments went unremarked upon—and perhaps even unnoticed—in much of Washington and elsewhere. The officer was, however, called to Washington to be thanked by the president for the work he had done in preventing multiple major terrorist attacks. Thus, in a modest ceremony in the Oval Office, in front of a small group of senior intelligence and government professionals, the president presented him a prestigious—and just a little bit gaudy—medal. During his remarks, the president marveled at how one man could accomplish so much. Displaying the attention to detail that had made him such a good president, he noted, "Some of the photographs you provided have almost simultaneous time and date stamps, but they were taken in totally different places. Your ability to be in multiple places at the same time amazes me. It's like magic. Tell me. Are you a magician?"

"A magician, Mister President? I have been called many things in my career. I think 'magician' will do just fine."

GIVE ME LIGHT

June 1991, outside a village in southwestern Syria

THE SUN DIPPED BELOW THE horizon, and darkness followed immediately. There was no twilight in the desert.

He was hidden under his desert-camouflage poncho, lying in a small crevasse where blown sand had drifted against a large rock. During the day he had struggled to breathe—the air was hot and dry, his nostrils caked with solidified mucus. His eyes were almost blind from reflected sunlight, even though he wore the latest in protective lenses. The heat of the hardpan sand and superhot rocks had blistered parts of his back and one of his elbows. His face was smeared with sun protection cream. The rest of his body was covered by a uniform, gloves, and a hood to protect his head and neck. The weapons and communications devices he carried had been the stuff of science fiction a decade ago, and he ardently wished that, in addition to these devices, someone had created a real-life special desert suit to recycle his body waste and aid his breathing. Perhaps something like the clothing worn by Frank Herbert's characters in

Dune. But his was not a messiah's mission, as had been that of Herbert's young protagonist, Paul Atreides; and his suit, while of a special material, neither recycled his body waste nor aided his breathing—hence the dried snot clogging his nostrils. He heard a slight whistle as he breathed in through his nose. That was exactly what he did not need—some sentry team investigating a whistling coming from the desert outskirts of the village.

But Frank Herbert and science fiction had not occupied his thoughts during the day. No, he had far greater questions to contemplate, including *why me?* Why had they selected him for this mission? He thought he knew at least part of the answer. They needed human eyes on the target, if target it was. All of their science-fiction-become-fact satellites and eavesdropping technology could not penetrate the complex they believed was in the village. It would take an experienced intelligence officer to make the decision to kill people.

How many people work in that complex? Five hundred? A thousand? More? Perhaps more, he thought, *perhaps more. They don't know how many; that's why they sent me. No, that's not why they sent me. In reality, they don't care how many people will die. They're only concerned about the implications of widening a war and perhaps bringing in European or Asian combatants. If the intelligence we're working on is correct, there may be North Koreans or Russians present. But are they rogue engineers, or do they represent an official presence? Still, if this is an assembly plant for warheads and they are creating dirty bombs with radiological waste…still…*

His attention was diverted by the sound of another truck turning onto the road into the complex from the village, which surrounded the facility on three sides. He looked at the small monitor that was hooked to an even smaller fiber-optic camera cable that snaked out from under his poncho. This was the fifth truck since he had crawled into position an hour before sunup this morning. Was it still today? It seemed more like a week.

Again he checked his radiation detector. Much higher readings here than in the desert. He had parachuted in last night, landing five miles from the village, and then had made his way on foot to the outskirts on the eastern edge. That's where the spy had said the complex was located. As soon as he'd landed, he'd taken a radiation reading, and he'd taken one again every mile or so on his ingress. At three miles the reading had begun to change. Now that he was only a little over three hundred meters from the complex, it was very high indeed. He had already identified the building where the majority of the activity was taking place. But still he wondered, *why me?*

In his forties, he was already a senior intelligence service officer, grade three, so it would be a senior officer who made the call on whether to destroy this complex and end the lives of these people. The need for senior eyes on the site might be the by-the-book reason he was there, but perhaps there was more. *Maybe they sent me because of my experience as the clandestine service's chief troubleshooter. Or maybe, just maybe, it's because someone actually believes the sobriquet my classmates hung on me during training: the Warrior Priest. Do they believe that having* someone who trained for the priesthood make the decision imbues that decision with a moral validation? He doubted it, believing that most of his colleagues tended to be amoral when it came to such decisions. "My side versus their side," usually seemed the primary criterion.

When darkness came he flipped down his night-vision goggles and edged his head and shoulders from under the poncho. He spread the fanlike antenna of his parabolic microphone and pointed it toward the buildings inside the fence three hundred meters in front of him. He only used one of the earbuds to listen. His other ear needed to be free to hear ambient sounds in case a patrol approached. He could hear the trucks without the parabolic microphone, but he wanted voices. Voices that would tell him what might be happening inside the complex and in which building, if any, the dirty warheads were being assembled. For that was his mission. Determine if the group was building dirty radioactive warheads for SCUD missiles. Missiles that might fall on Israeli cities or US and coalition troops in Kuwait and Saudi Arabia. Or perhaps they were constructing a truck bomb full of hospital and industrial radioactive waste that could go off in Tel Aviv, or Jeddah, or perhaps even Cairo, where it could be blamed on the Israelis. *How many thousands might die?* he asked himself. *How many?*

Still, do I have the right to kill a thousand to save ten thousand or even a hundred thousand? What is the ratio that justifies killing?

He checked his watch. It was now just past midnight. The complex was dark except for a few security lamps. The plan to destroy it, should it need to be destroyed, was set for two o'clock. Less than two more hours. A bomber using a commercial flight call sign, altitude, and airway would drop three large devices that would follow the infrared laser beam he would use to illuminate the complex. The devices would carry thermite charges. The thought was that thermite would destroy the radiological waste by incinerating it. Conventional bombs would only spread the radiation over a large area. So there would be no explosions. Still, the smoke from the fires would carry radiation up into the winds and then perhaps for hundreds of miles. *How many innocents will die?* This thought repeated itself, becoming every other thought that crossed his mind as he considered the potential target.

Does this site really have to be destroyed? Can't we just destroy the trucks as they depart to deliver the warheads? He had begun to ask the question because he was now fairly sure the spy's information had been correct. There was no other logical reason for such a complex. *How many innocents will die? Just in the village alone there must be a thousand or more who will be exposed to the smoke.* He debated with himself. He rationalized, but his rationalization was weak. He knew it.

He checked his laser designator. The battery indicated a full charge. He turned on his small radio and placed it in the listening mode. His responses would only be clicks on the microphone button. It was not his job to report. When the bomber asked for illumination, he was to click the button twice to indicate a "no go" and four times to indicate a "go." He placed the illuminator on the edge of his small hiding place. It faced the largest of the three buildings.

How many will die? Is that the question I should be asking? Perhaps the more correct question is—how many will live? As time dwindled, the debate became a heated one in his mind with one side screaming at the other, *How many will die?* Answered by a clearer, calmer voice: *But how many will live?*

There was a buzz as the radio came to life.

"Give me light," the bombardier demanded. "Give me light."

From Dark to Light to Dark

April 1972, North Vietnam

TRAN USED A SMALL FLASHLIGHT to find his team's way through the forest to the road he knew was two hundred meters west of the helicopter-landing site where he had just been "dropped." They pushed their small motorbikes, but once they reached the road, they would start them up and ride toward the next village to the north. They would stop five kilometers outside the village so as not to enter during the middle of the night. Doing so would be suspicious, and suspicion was something spies always needed to avoid. They would find a place off the road and sleep late. Tran would once again go over their cover story with his agents, and then they would enter the village sometime after noon.

"From Dark to Light to Dark" originally appeared as chapter 5 in the author's second novel, *Flying Blind*.

Tran took the first watch as they bedded down for the rest of the night. As he sat staring into the darkness, he wondered if this would be the mission where something went wrong. "No," he said sotto voce, "not *if* something goes wrong. Something *always* goes wrong, but in the past I've always managed to walk or talk my way out of the situation. What I really mean is…is this the time I won't be able to handle the situation?" He loved the dark, but he hated the waiting.

Danny Tran, as he was known to his college classmates at Yale, was one of the first Vietnamese graduates of that august institution. But he wasn't really Vietnamese. He had been born in Vietnam and had spent the first eleven years of his life there. He was fluent in the language, and he certainly looked Vietnamese, but he didn't think of himself as Vietnamese.

His father and grandfather had been very successful businessmen in pre–World War II French Indochina, but after the war his father had understood that Ho Chi Minh would eventually come to power and had relocated the family from Hanoi to the United States. He had meant to go to France, where he held citizenship, but an opportunity to become the director of raw rubber acquisition for a major American tire and rubber company had presented itself, and he had taken it.

So, eleven-year-old Tran Duc Dan moved with his family to Ohio, where he had taken to the culture like he had been born into it. He became Danny Tran, a stalwart of his private school's wrestling and baseball teams. At Yale he became an all-Ivy wrestler as well as an honorable mention all-American second baseman. In college, during the ramp up of the Cold War, he had studied all things Russian, as well as political science in general. With his native Vietnamese and French, and a mastery of Russian gained during his four years at Yale, he had been a natural candidate when the CIA talent scouts at Yale began charting the progress of potential initiates for the recently formed clandestine agency.

His first inkling of his recruitment had come during drinks and dinner at his Russian professor's home. At first he thought he might be a candidate for one of the secret societies like Skull and Bones. But after a few meetings where he was progressively handed off from one person to another, it became clear the society that was interested in him was very secret, but much different than Skull and Bones. It was a secret society where, if your membership became known, you just might be on the short list to be assassinated or imprisoned and tortured. But he was Danny Tran, a true-blue American from his flattop haircut to his Bass Weejun loafers. His country needed him.

And it had used him. With the appropriate forged Vietnamese or French documents, he could get close to Russian and Eastern European diplomats and trade representatives. He wasn't looking so much to recruit them as to identify which of them were using their status to cover their real purpose of being themselves spies or spymasters. It was the classic matchup of spy versus spy. Once identified, the Russian or Pole or Czech would be tracked, and when possible, false and misleading information would be passed their way. Danny would also attempt to identify their targets for recruitment, and possibly the agents they had already recruited and were meeting and directing. Then appropriate covert active measures would be taken in respect to those spies as well. It was the stuff of James Bond novels. No, actually, it was much better than James Bond novels. It was real life, and in the real-life spy business, reputation, credibility, and even life itself were hazarded. The secret wasn't that this sort of thing occurred, the secret was in knowing who was involved and what, exactly, they were doing. Over the years his cover had held, and so far he had not been identified as an American operative. Thus he remained in the field and had not moved to CIA Headquarters at Langley.

But now they needed him to try and confirm if, where, and how North Vietnam might be hiding US prisoners of war. It was thought all US POWs had been moved into a prison in downtown Hanoi after the failed Son Tay raid of 1970, but intelligence anomalies and bits and pieces of information reaching CIA Headquarters indicated there might still be individual POWs held outside Hanoi. Also, there was a possibility that Russians were involved in the activity and that some of the POWs might actually have been transferred to Russian control. Find out. This was his mission.

He wondered about the two neophyte agents in his charge. Sister and brother, they had extended family in some of the nearby villages. Their cover story was that they had been living in Hanoi, but bombing had damaged their apartment building, and they wanted to be safe. Children of a Vietnamese father and French mother, they had begun life in the middle class of business families in Hanoi, but with the ascendance of the Communist Party, the family had dropped further and further down the ladder of respectability as Communist Party members began to supplant the Indo-French members of

Vietnamese society. The brother was educated, even having a year of university, but had become a cobbler because he wasn't a member of the Communist Party. The sister was an excellent tailor, and both carried the rudimentary tools of their trades in a large collapsible basket she held while riding sidesaddle on the pillion of his motorbike. They were good at keeping secrets. For many years they had managed a semisuccessful existence in Hanoi.

Tran had found the two in a displaced persons camp in Laos. They had been captured crossing the border with badly forged documents that proclaimed they had family in South Vietnam whom they were trying to reach. At least, they reasoned, they had made it out of North Vietnam—but now Tran had convinced them to return. Not because he had somehow persuaded them North Vietnam would lose the war, nor had he promised legal entry into South Vietnam. No, he held out the ultimate entitlement—access to the United States. It had taken a little to-ing and fro-ing with Langley, but he had persuaded the policy people that if answering the questions surrounding American POWs was both urgent and significant, then two more immigrants into the United States would be worth the cost. The agreement was that the two had to remain in North Vietnam for at least a year, traveling between rural areas, villages, and cities to seek out information on POWs and Russians. That done, they would be resettled in the United States—unless, of course, some other mission could be identified where their particular skills and nationality would be of use. Tran, needless to say, did not share this other option with them. No sense in worrying any further ahead than tomorrow, when they might at any moment encounter someone who could make their only future prison and death.

Tran's cover was that of a researcher for Russian interests in how much agricultural production could be increased by introducing tractors into the agricultural collectives. He possessed certain Russian and Vietnamese documents that would pass all but the most rigid of inspections in Hanoi or Moscow. Such documents allowed him to discuss the labor situation with farmers in what were very loosely run farm collectives. During his first two trips, he had learned that the collectives used more than 80 to 90 percent of what they produced for local needs. Only 10 to 20 percent of what they grew ended up headed for Hanoi or Haiphong. That certainly wasn't what the Communist Party intended.

His minions waited outside town while he circled around and entered the village from the north. In midafternoon, they entered from the east.

In that first village, the man and the woman inquired about possible family members, but there was no one who remembered their father...perhaps in the next village. They remained two days before moving on. The man repaired some shoes and sandals, the woman did some mending of dresses and winter coats for members of the collective leaders' families. He asked if perhaps there were Europeans about who might need shoes or boots repaired. She asked if there were any foreign ladies who might need dresses sewn. No one remembered any foreigners having been in the village for years, unless of course, you counted the Communists from Hanoi who came to tell them they had become free, but that freedom meant they had to give part of their produce—give, mind you, not sell—to the people of Hanoi and Haiphong who protected them from the French and others who sought to exploit them. No one in the village remembered ever feeling threatened by the French; the French had not asked them to give their produce away but rather had been eager to buy some of it. It didn't make sense to the villagers that now they had to work other people's land—the land they had previously owned now belonging to the collective. No sense at all, but no, they had not seen any foreigners, French or otherwise, for years. Perhaps more to the east, over near some of the former French rubber plantations.

The man and the woman traded work for food, although they did have sufficient đồng in coins and a few bills to buy things if there was no work available. In the second village, there was a rumor of foreigners who had been in a camp in the forest off the road to the north, but a quick ride out the road by Tran brought no success. On the eighth day, there was a road checkpoint they had to negotiate. They had learned of the checkpoint in the village before leaving, and Tran had instructed the brother and sister to go in front of him. When he came upon the checkpoint he was concerned when he saw their motorbike leaned against the guard hut. Yet when he stopped to show his papers to the guard he saw the couple inside the hut. The man was mending a pair of officer's boots, and the woman was sewing up what appeared to be a tear in a shirt. He waited for them two kilometers down the road, just as earlier he had instructed them to do for him. After an hour, he worried. After two hours he worried more, but after three a dust cloud appeared up the road, and shortly thereafter they joined him. They were almost giddy with success. They had earned a few thousand đồng and learned much about Russians who had been in the area but were no longer there.

In the next village the young man asked one of the elders if perhaps there were people of quality in the area who might need leather work or sewing done. "People of quality, you ask," the elder replied. "We are farmers forced into groups with people with whom we would formerly have had no association. The only 'people of quality' now are those who are Party members. No, there are no people of quality hereabouts."

The reply did not surprise the cobbler, but he was careful not to express sympathy for the elder's comments because in Hanoi, he had learned the Communist Party had spies everywhere, and to speak against the Party could earn you a prison sentence. It was this culture he and his sister had tried to escape.

On the ninth day, Tran showed the couple the site where he would reappear on his next visit. That visit would not be for several weeks since the couple could now serve as the eyes and ears that he himself had been on previous missions. When he left, they were to keep traveling through the region seeking information about potential POW sites and Russian presence. If they discovered any factual knowledge about the presence of POWs, they were to use the communication device he left with them. Concealed in the small, hand-operated sewing machine the girl carried in the basket was a simple burst transmitter. By stringing out a spool of wire thread for an antenna, they could send a series of bursts on a single frequency. Three bursts meant "need to meet." Four bursts meant "have definite information on POWs." Five bursts meant "trouble." They had memorized where and when Tran would appear if they sent him a signal.

On the tenth day, Tran hugged both of them, buoyed their spirits by reminding them of their future in the United States, and then rode off toward the site where the black bird would meet him at midnight.

At midnight plus two, one of the crewmen aboard the helicopter rolled Tran's motorbike up the ramp while Tran strapped himself into the sling seat. At midnight plus four, the black bird lifted into the tops of the trees.

Tran spent the entire return flight reviewing all he had done, the little he had gained, and the prodigious perils he and his agents had faced. By the time the crew dropped him off at his secret rendezvous site in Thailand, he was no longer Tran the spymaster, but Danny Tran, American through and through, willing to hazard all dangers in order to return safely those who had been captured. How appropriate, he thought, that the helicopter was being flown by an air rescue crew whose motto was "That Others May Live."

OLD TIMES

February 2014, Paris

HE TOOK THE METRO TEN stops down the embankment, then walked four blocks through the February slush. Paris could be cold and ugly in the winter. The slush came up over the soles of his well-scuffed brown leather oxfords. He turned up the collar of his thigh-length wool coat in a futile attempt to keep the wind off. Like the rest of Paris, the coat was dark blue. Neither the collar nor his beret did anything for his ears, which had begun to burn in the cold wind. He loosened his scarf, pulling it up over his ears. As he did so, he glanced—just for a second—at the street behind him.

He remembered the corner, but checked the street sign to make sure. He looked down the small, mean-looking lane and stepped around the corner. He waited; no one turned behind him. He did not feel followed, nor had he seen anyone since he started his journey earlier that afternoon.

Midway down the block he came to the bistro. It did not appear much changed, although the sign appeared to have been repainted. *Café Le Coq Rouge* it said under what was now the silhouette of a bright-red rooster but had then been a faded, rust-colored shadow.

The tables were small and close together, but there were a few along the wall near the back that were a bit farther apart. They were on the periphery and didn't get the full sound from the band on the stage. *Band?* Well, it was actually a trio playing. A violin, an accordion, and a bassist-cum-percussionist who— in addition to his bass viol—had a variety of washboards, cymbals, and other such accoutrements. They were doing a good job of "Tango Jealousy." They weren't Galliano and Piazzolla, but they were OK.

He undid the buttons on his coat but kept it—and his beret—on. The air hung heavy and thick with Gauloise smoke. With only a little imagination, you could almost see the music making its way through the room, pushing the smoke in rhythmic patterns. He sat at one of the tables in the rear. One where he could see the door. His two-day growth of beard, blue denim shirt, and well-washed jeans seemed right for the occasion. He placed the folded copy of the *Financial Times* on the table, its pink paper barely visible in the dimness of the cafe.

A waiter appeared and asked if he wanted a menu. "No," he said. "Just a cognac."

His French was not Parisian. It was tainted with the patois of North Africa. A pied-noir, the waiter would think. He watched the door. A couple came in. *Could they be surveillance? Maybe. Where would they sit?* When they went to the other side of the stage, and out of his direct line of sight, he relaxed. Good surveillants would place themselves somewhere they could keep eyes on him. No, his sixth sense was telling him he was clean.

Two couples made staccato steps that transitioned into a series of legato movements—stretching themselves across the small dance floor while weaving their legs in and out to the tango. It was a dance demanding teamwork and advance knowledge about what the lead was going to do. If your partner didn't have such knowledge you would embarrass yourself, stepping on her foot, and she yours—and then, down you would go. Arms and legs askew, you would look up from the floor and, if you were smart, join in the laughter of the other patrons. Lots of practice at home was required to carry off a good tango, even in a working-class café like this one.

When the waiter brought his cognac, he took the glass from the table and quickly downed it. He put the glass back on the waiter's tray, threw a ten-euro note behind it and ordered another.

He watched the door.

Sometimes the agent had been late. After all, he had responsibilities. He did not get to Paris that frequently. Sometimes he had been as much as three-quarters of an hour late. Patrons came, couples, singles, once a threesome. But not his man.

A banker. He had been a banker. Not like the other spies he handled. Not a military officer, not a government underminister, not a wannabe assassin, not an actual assassin. This man was just a banker who held and moved money for all sorts of people and companies. When he had obtained the accounts for the Palestinian Liberation Organization, it had initially been a coup, but then it had become more of a burden. A burden to the banker both professionally and personally. He couldn't refuse their business if he wanted to, since one did not say no to the PLO.

When an intelligence service had come to him, interested in information about the PLO, the Tunisian had at first resisted, but after much work on the spymaster's part, he had reluctantly agreed. The spymaster had convinced him it was safe. The bank was in Tunis, and there would be no contact with the intelligence service except here in Paris. Still the banker had always been nervous.

The spymaster moved the pink newspaper closer to the edge of the table. It was the safety signal. Were the banker to enter now, he would know it was safe to cross the room and sit at the table. If there was no newspaper, or the newspaper wasn't pink, the banker would go to the bar, order a drink, and then leave. He, too, would be carrying a copy of the pink newspaper—only his would have lists inserted between the folds. Lists of where and when and to whom the PLO was sending money, and from whence money into the accounts was coming. The exchange of pink papers could have been made in a brief encounter, a brush-pass or even a timed dead drop, but this agent needed to be reassured and encouraged—thus the face-to-face meetings in out-of-the-way cafés in a section of Paris that tourists and bankers generally avoided.

He watched the door. A man with a long overcoat and a homburg hat entered. Could this be his banker? No, someone from across the dance floor waved him to a table.

It had always been and still was a safe meeting venue. He himself had flown into Paris only occasionally—alerted by a postcard mailed to an address in Switzerland. A dead-letter drop they called it. The banker mailed the letter to the Swiss address, and "they" let the spymaster know when the banker would be in Paris. The meetings were always set for early evenings at one of four bistros that rotated on a list. He always had hoped the banker would not go to the wrong café. Certainly, the banker would not. They had done this for more than two years, and the banker had never missed a meeting. He had been late, but he had never missed.

The man watched the door, but the banker did not come. He had another cognac, his third. It had been more than an hour. Ten more minutes. He could afford only ten more minutes. He, too, had responsibilities this evening.

It had been his plan to tell the banker that, safe as they had been, they must stop meeting as a precaution. Other intelligence sources had determined the PLO knew that someone—someone who knew beforehand where the money was going—was tipping off Western intelligence regarding the PLO's arms and explosives purchases. That Western intelligence operatives rigged the rifles so that they would blow up when fired, or they modified explosives to detonate prematurely or not detonate at all. The PLO was investigating, and the banker needed to lie low. But the banker had not come. He had never missed a meeting before, but he had not come that time. Had the spymaster himself been too late? Not for the meeting, but too late to save the banker?

He buttoned his coat, took up the pink newspaper, and slipped it into the side pocket of his coat. He pushed open the café door and left, pursued by as much Gauloise smoke as the music could push out behind him. He leaned backward against the wind, pulling his collar and scarf up around his ears. The wind now thrust him down the street as if to hasten his departure.

At the hotel he passed through the side lobby so as not to attract the attention of the doorman or desk clerks. When he reached the suite, his wife greeted him.

"Oh, there you are! I thought we might have to be late to the dinner. I was just about to call our hosts, but here you are."

"Yes, here I am," he said, taking off his beret, coat, and scarf. "Here I am."

His wife twirled in front of him; her gown blossomed out. She smiled. "We'll have great fun. Dinner and dancing. Will you tango with me?"

"Tango?" he asked absentmindedly. "Tango? Of course."

"Where have you been all afternoon and evening? My goodness, you look a real scoundrel. And you smell like..." She thought. "Like a barroom." She surveyed his outfit while pinching her nostrils with thumb and forefinger.

"Oh, just went out to see an old friend. Well, he was more of an old business acquaintance, really."

"Did you have a good conversation?" she asked.

"He never came."

"Oh, I'm sorry. But I'm glad you're back. We're going to have a wonderful evening. Just like old times."

He looked hard at himself in the mirror behind the door. Yes, the shirt was right as were the jeans. The shoes were working-class too. The coat, the beret, the newspaper—all were correct. The only thing different was his hair—which was now completely gray (it had been dark then)—and his eyes. Yes, although his eyes were the same green-blue, they looked more—very much more—old, and sadder. How long had it been? Twenty-five, no, more like thirty years. Too long to hope, but not to remember.

SANCTUARY

2012, Arab Africa

I am searching for God. I have been searching for God since I was twenty-one years old. I have been to five thousand three hundred and twelve churches, mosques, synagogues, and temples. I have traveled to seventy-four countries and more than two thousand cities, villages, and rural hamlets. At first I spoke with priests and rabbis, imams and yogis, but they offered nothing but words. They all explained the nature of God to me as they understood it, but they could not answer my question: "If God is truly omnipotent and omniscient then how can his nature be fixed?" My journal abounds with failed explanations. When they were unable to answer my questions, I ceased to seek their knowledge, for I understood they had bound themselves and God with dogma. I searched on my own for the presence of God.

I have read hundreds of books on theology and philosophy. I have explored Socrates, Plato, Democritus, Zeno, Epictetus, Confucius, Augustine, Lucretius, Moore, Lao Tzu, Law, Smith, de Montaigne, Kant, Nietzsche, Lightfoot, Buber, Tillich, Camus, and a host of others, whose names you might not recognize. Of these I find most reasonable those who suggest practical philosophies for daily lives rather than those who explore the abstract. I also find it difficult to place any value in those who did not live the philosophies they championed. For example: Rousseau was a scoundrel. He hid from the church and fathered five children out of wedlock, all of whom were turned over to state-run orphanages, and none of whom ever reached adulthood. Yet his *The Social Contract* is honored as a fundamental document for the democratically minded. It falls into the "Do as I say, not as I do" category of undertakings.

Personally I favor de Montaigne's "Unable to govern events, I govern myself" as the most usable of the lot. Of course, that advice can be traced back through a number of other philosophers to Zeno and the Stoics. Combined with the admonition I have found in most every religion, "Treat others as you would be treated," it forms an excellent base from which to work. Still, I long to find God. I know he's here somewhere; I've seen the evidence of his presence. I have seen miracles, so of course I believe in them. I would tell you about them, but you'd simply dismiss them as coincidence or happenstance. Miracles are mostly like funny situations; you have to be there to appreciate them. In retelling they lose their magic. So I know God is here somewhere. I just haven't seen or spoken with him.

I'm in a town in Arab Africa. I've come to take pictures of their small pyramids and explore Sufi Islam. At least that's what I told the immigration officer at the airport. Actually I've come to deal with an individual who, left unchecked, will become a major problem for the region and perhaps the world. But unlike so many past potential threats to order and security, he will not be allowed to flourish. If only someone had done this before. Think what the present condition of the world might be if Hitler had died an undistinguished death in 1924, or Stalin in 1918 or...well, you understand. There's a long list of people who, if they had been removed from the scene before they became demagogues, the world would be a much different place.

You're probably thinking I'm some sort of government assassin. Or perhaps I represent a group of very smart people who want to save the world. But you are wrong. I answer to no one but myself. You see, I am an amateur assassin. I used to be a professional spy, but now I'm retired. I travel the world, removing potential threats before they leave the destruction and death that follows in the wake of such demonic demagogues. It's something useful I do while I search for God.

There have been places I thought I could feel God's presence. Certain churches when empty seemed to be full of God, but those same churches full of people were devoid of the presence. Today I'm sitting in an Anglican church that is surrounded by mosques. The church is a holdover from the days of British imperialism. It's large and remarkably cool, given the hundred-plus degree temperature just outside the doors. But I feel no presence of God here, just as I felt no presence of God in the mosque next door. There are some places I visit where not only do I not feel a lingering presence of God, but I feel as if a barrier has been thrust up between God and man. These places, regardless of how large they are, feel claustrophobic.

I sit in a pew at the back of the church. With the open doors and windows—the church has no air-conditioning—the outside sounds of an overpopulated city intrude, as do the fumes from cars that in Europe or the United States would be taken off the streets for safety purposes but that here are upper-class transportation. I think of my approach to my target. I am not a messy assassin. I don't use guns or knives. My methods give my targets a chance to consider their mortality, and hopefully, as they do, they recognize the consequences of their actions upon their lives. Somehow I doubt they actually ever do recognize the link between their actions and their untimely ends, but I don't doubt that as the end nears, many reach out to God, offering all manner of deals if he will but spare their lives.

You may think it strange, perhaps even eerily weird, that I sit in a church and contemplate the death of a human being. But, in fact, isn't that what church is about, the death of a human being? Not so in a mosque, but then one can't sit in a mosque. They don't have chairs or pews, and at sixty-seven my knees are not up to sitting cross-legged on the floor. I often find a church in which to sit awhile before beginning my approach to my targets.

I use a slow-acting poison of my own making. It is a nicotine- and ricin-based derivative mixed with…well…I don't think I should share the secret ingredient, for you or others might use it for nefarious purposes. Anyway, its effects are a slow weakening of the target's muscles, nausea, and slight dizziness; and finally, the heart stops. It only takes a drop to be lethal, but because it is slow acting, there is a forty-eight to seventy-two-hour window between exposure and any major onset of the effects. I have two delivery methods: either actually touching my target or a directed droplet launched from a compressed air device mounted on my camera. There is no antidote, so I must be extremely careful that I do not poison myself. Because of the risk associated with engaging the target, I find myself often contemplating my own death while seated in the church. Today is no different. I have chosen to use the touch method where I will shake hands with the target. On my middle finger will be a plastic bandage that appears to be a Band-Aid. In fact, it is a plastic sleeve that fits over my finger, the pad of which has a miniscule beadlike capsule with the poison. As I grab the target's hand my finger extends up his wrist where I press down, rupturing the bead and delivering the poison. It is a simple yet dangerous task. Most of my risks involve remembering not to touch exposed skin, either mine or someone not the target, as I disengage and depart the area. And that's all I have to say about my methods. I don't see why you need to know how I do it. Only that I do it to protect others, you included.

Yes, yes, I know. How dare I take on the role of judge, jury, and executioner? Still, you must remember we live in a world where some countries allow sixteen-year-old girls to terminate lives and where mass killings and attempted genocide are not uncommon occurrences. At least I've got experience behind me, having lived and dealt with miscreants and demagogues for scores of years. At first I gave great thought to the metaphysical consequences of my actions but, like with the holy men, after a while I stopped tormenting myself about the correctness of my efforts. The likelihood that I am terminating another Hitler, Stalin, Idi Amin, or Vlad the Impaler is great, while the likelihood that those sixteen-year-old girls and mass killers are terminating another Einstein, Washington, Mother Teresa—or perhaps even a Jesus or Buddha—is at least within the realm of possibility. Besides, if God thought I was doing the wrong thing, he would have told me by now. He's had enough chances.

My target today is attending a reception given by a non-governmental organization at a large hotel. I have been in town long enough to have wangled myself an invitation. Foreigners aren't plentiful here, so it is easy to fall in with one of these groups of Americans, Europeans, and Australians who some-how believe themselves to be doing God's work. Still, they are working for the people my target seeks to oppress if he is given the opportunity, so I too am working for them.

I reach the hotel at the beginning of the reception. I do not want to miss an opportunity. I linger at the drinks table nearest the main entrance to the ballroom. It is laden with glasses of fruit juice and doughy pastries that contain cold lamb meat. I sip my mango juice and wait, occasionally speaking with one of my new acquaintances but never taking my eyes from the door. The room fills with dishdashas, thobes, caftans, and cheaply made western suits. All males, no females. As an Australian engages me in conversation, I maneuver him so I can look over his shoulder at the entrance.

Commotion! I hear yelling in Arabic, then gunshots, then more gunshots from just outside the entrance. People try to run into the hall while others are trying to run out. I don't move, holding my position between the table and the wall. After the initial crush, the door clears as people flee the ballroom through other exits. I edge my way to the ballroom entrance.

In the lobby of the hotel lies the body of my target, three distinct red holes in the front of his enamel-white thobe. His turban is still on his head. His eyes stare upward. Ten feet away lies another body, surrounded by men with pistols and machine guns. This body has a bare head and holds a pistol in its hand. It wears black trousers and a long-sleeved white shirt, the uniform of the hotel's waiters.

I make my way from the hotel, stopping once again at the church. I sit and remove the plastic sleeve from my finger while wondering how I could have missed in my research that my target had moved up sufficiently to find himself on the assassination list of a professional group. Or did the young man act alone? Did he have some personal animosity for the target? Was he or his family wrongly treated? This, however, is not my concern. Let CNN sort it out.

I do not feel cheated, for I am now free to move on to my next target, a firebrand anarchist who, left unchecked, will gain a significant following in a year or so.

I close my eyes and listen. No, God is not present in this church. And while it is not a sanctum for the soul, it does make a passable sanctuary from the immediacies of the outside world.

I Love You Still

January 2015, Ohio

SHE HAS NEVER HEARD OF the African person whose head is depicted on the three deep-purple, rather ostentatious stamps at the upper right of the box. The return address is not all legible. There is a name and there are some numbers in a foreign script, maybe Arabic, but she is not sure. The box looks as if it might have been a box for Christmas-sized greeting cards in its first life, although perhaps it is a little deep for that. It rattles slightly when shaken. She has to go to the kitchen to find a knife with which to cut the heavy twine that binds the brown paper wrapping. There is a greasy substance on the brown paper as if someone had spilled olive oil.

She cuts the twine and unwraps the paper from the box. There is some black block printing on the back of the heavy paper which includes an address in Nigeria. The box had not been for cards, but for cartridges. Caliber 5.62 is printed on the box's top.

Who on earth would be sending her a cartridge box from a foreign country?

With some difficulty she lifts the top from the box. Inside is a folded letter, and beneath the letter what looks like military medals and some small photographs. There is an expensive-looking fountain pen, and at the bottom of the box, there is a smallish diary-like book. She takes everything out, laying the items one by one on the cooking island in the middle of her kitchen. Eight medals with ribbons attached, three photographs, a fountain pen, the letter, and the notebook.

She takes up the first of the photographs. In a four-by-six print, four soldiers stand next to a jeep. The faces are tan. All hold weapons and wear soft, wide-brimmed hats. Two are wearing shorts, and the other two have on khaki field pants; all wear boots. Written on the back, in a hand that momentarily seems familiar, is, "Me and the boys."

A second picture, another four by six, is of the park near what had been the center of her town before the malls were built. Taken in the spring, there are roses and other bright flowers in the foreground and the green grass of the expansive lawn behind. The trees on the edge make it seem like a postcard advertising what had once been a picturesque small-town tableau.

The third picture is a wallet-size portrait photograph of her as a college senior. She wears a black, low-cut gown. It was her sorority yearbook photograph. On the back is written, "All my love, Sheila. XXXOOO."

"How strange," she murmurs.

All three photographs have a crusty red-brown stain that has soaked into the paper.

She takes up the first photograph and looks closely at one of the men standing in the middle. Yes, it is him—older, but still him. She has not thought of him in years. Once or twice people in town mentioned his name, but again, not for years. Someone said he had died in a foreign country while doing some sort of work for a foreign government. "This is completely unexpected," she says aloud. She opens the letter:

Sheila,

You don't know me, but I am a friend of Frank's. We have been friends for years, going from struggle to struggle. I know he did not write you because he felt you did not need to be burdened by thinking of him, and particularly he did not want to cause an uneasiness in your marriage. But please know that he thought of you constantly. You were his ideal, the reason he fought to do right.

I have enclosed his last diary. I burned the others, although they would have made an excellent book. You have no idea how much Frank has done to bring order out of chaos in this part of the world.

He was killed two weeks ago in an action against Boko Haram here in Northern Nigeria. We were contracted by the Nigerian government to try to catch the leader of the movement, Abubakr Shekau, and return as many of the stolen girls as we could recover. We sent thirty of the girls to Abuja last month, but we did not succeed in capturing Abubakr Shekau.

Frank was our leader, and I don't know if the rest of us of have the drive or the heart to continue now that he is dead.

I was to burn all his things, since he always said he no longer had a home but lived wherever he fell asleep the night before. However, when I read his journals I discovered an unfinished poem, and the poet in me could not help but think that somehow a story of unrequited love must have a happy ending. Everyone should have someone to mark their passing. I thought you should know how he felt.

The medals are from thankful governments for Frank's work protecting the weak from the strong. The sheep from the hyenas, if you will. You'll see if you read his journal. He became a great man. I took the liberty of finishing the poem by adding the last two stanzas. It isn't Tennyson, but it is expressive. I hope I have not opened old wounds and that I have done the right thing in sending you these relics of Frank's life. Do not grieve too much; Frank would not have wanted that.

> Frank's Friend
> Eduardo Xavier Sento
> Village of Nguru
> Yobe Province
> Nigeria

She reads the poem:

I Love You Still

I love you still.
Though you have chosen someone else,
I love you still.
Did you know before you chose?
But now you never can—
And near or far,
I love you still.

Too near I cannot stay,
And yet I dare not go too far
Unless some respite
For unrequited love I find,
I love you still.

So now my pursuit of love ends—
How do I live my life?
Shall I seek fame, fortune, danger?
Yes, danger—that's the thing!
Adrenaline dulls love's ecstasy and pain
So I will embrace danger as my love,
Although I love you still.

And so he did,
From hostile desert to embittered cityscape
Always seeking righteous causes.

Follow me! he shouted,
You cannot live forever!
His comrades, wary of his love of danger
And his constancy to right,
Yet he loved it so.

And then the sand clumped as his life spilled out.
His open eyes a distant memory sought
Follow me! his comrades heard
But as the wasteland soaked up his blood
He whispered so that only God could hear,
I love you still.

She crushes the letter in her hand. Stepping on the lever to open the kitchen trashcan, she drops the letter into the container and follows it by sweeping with her hand the other items from the island counter.

"It would only complicate things," she says aloud. "He was cute, but it wasn't as if I ever *really* loved him."

Then, stooping, she reaches into the open can, draws out the pen, and places it in her pocket. "No sense in throwing away a perfectly good pen," she says to herself. "After all, it is a Mont Blanc."

JUSTICE

July 1993, Evin Prison in Northwest Tehran

"I AM NOT GUILTY! As Allah is my witness, *I am not guilty!*"

He held a trembling hand over his fast-beating heart to show his honesty. He could hear that heart throbbing in his ears. He felt it in his chest, but it beat its quick rhythm into his head as well. His eyes felt as if they might be forced from their sockets by the pressure.

It was humid and hot in the room. He could smell his sweat. He did not like the smell, because he knew it was the smell of fear, and it clung to him and saturated his shirt and the crotch of his pants. He did not know why he was here. He did not know of what he was not guilty, just that he was not guilty.

"Reza, Reza, Reza. Calm yourself. Of course you're not guilty. I know you're not guilty. Even the prosecutor knows you're not guilty, but these things have to take their course. The court found you guilty, but I'm sure the ayatollah reviewing your case will be lenient, and we can always appeal to the grand ayatollah."

"Court? What court? I've not been in a court. Leniency for what? For what charges? When did this court meet? Who was on it? Why am I even here in Evin? I have done nothing wrong! I have operations that must be serviced in Europe. I want to speak immediately with the chief of my section in the ministry."

He had had nothing to eat or drink for the better part of two days. He felt light-headed, and the more he spoke, the more the room seemed to close down in its dimness, and the more tunnel-like his vision became. His breathing was fast—not so fast as his heart, but fast. He had to gain control. He reached for the table edge to steady himself and found the hard wooden chair. He sat. He placed the palms of his hands over his eyes as if to push them back into his head. He tried to concentrate on getting his breathing under control. He realized he was hyperventilating. He moved his hands into a cup over his nose and mouth to breathe his own carbon dioxide. After a few minutes, he would be all right. But who was this man in front of him?

"Who are you?" His heart slowed a little, his vision widened again, but the room remained a room of shadows from the one dirty ceiling light. He looked up into the face of his visitor. "Who are you?" He asked again.

"I'm Farrock Mazdaki, your lawyer."

"My lawyer? Of what am I accused?"

"Treason. You are accused of treason in that you have used your position in the Ministry of Information to set up personal bank accounts in foreign countries. That you have stolen funds belonging to the Islamic Republic and deposited them into these foreign accounts. You are further charged with lying about your foreign contacts in that you are keeping several foreign mistresses and supporting them with money belonging to the Islamic Republic. There are other charges but they all add up to you have betrayed the trust of the Republic and are, therefore, a traitor."

His heart started to increase its rate again and he gulped air as he half rose from his chair only to find himself falling back into it.

He yelled at the lawyer, "Traitor? Me? A traitor? I am not a traitor! *I am not a traitor!* I am *not* a trait..." He sank onto the chair, his head in his hands, his lungs seeking air, the pounding in his head greater than before. His vision closed down, and he knew surely that he would collapse. But no, he remained conscious.

The smell of his fear had reached the lawyer, who drew a handkerchief from his coat pocket and put it to his nose. The reek of the sweat, mingled with the stench of the strong urine of a dehydrated man that came from the can in the corner, almost overcame him. That the prisoner had enough moisture left to sweat so profusely surprised the lawyer, but in a way he had become used to such odors defending traitors to the republic. Still, he feared for the cloth of his suit. Would he smell of fear and urine when he returned to his office? He stood closer to the door.

The door opened, and a tall man, wide at the shoulders with a bald head and a full beard, entered the room. He wore an ill-fitting suit, but his presence commanded respect. "I am Deputy Minister Faraj. This man worked for me."

The lawyer had seen many deputy ministers, and some ministers as well, so he was not impressed, although physically he did feel a little intimidated. Still, the thought that only last year he had seen a deputy minister sitting in the prisoner's chair kept him from being afraid of the big man.

"Ah, yes," said the lawyer, "his immediate supervisor. You're the one the court asked about when they wanted to know how long this man was allowed to betray the Republic." Too late he realized this was also the man in charge of the unacknowledged Department 311, the department that was believed to be responsible for handling the cases of political dissidents and threats to the regime. It was sometimes referred to in whispers as the Bureau of Political Assassinations. This thought made him begin to sweat himself, and his sweat too was the sweat of fear. "I mean, of course, you are the man who turned him in. That is what I meant." He stumbled with the explanation and was only too glad to leave the room as the large man motioned him out.

The prisoner lifted his head from his hands. "You turned me in? Your best operative? You turned me in? For what? I have done nothing. I am innocent." His voice was weak, for this man whose broad shadow now overhung the table had been his hope, his redeemer.

"Reza, I had no choice. We have a new agent. You know him. He provided you cover in Europe with Bank Melli. He transferred funds into your operational account. You stayed in his apartment in Zurich.

"Last fall we dangled him in front of the American CIA, and they quickly recruited him as an agent, but he is ours, a double agent. It is through him that we know the Americans suspect that you are one of our operatives. They have asked him to gather information on you and have provided him with intelligence they have already collected about you. They showed him photographs of you and foreign women. They provided him with the numbers of bank accounts that you have in European banks that we know nothing about. Reza, have you been skimming the cream off the top of your operational funds?"

"No, I would never do such a thing! Please, Istad!" he pleaded to his master. "There is some mistake. You know me. I am loyal. I have done everything that has been asked of me. I am loyal to the revolution." His voice remained weak, but he hoped to convince his master that he would never turn his back on the Islamic Revolution.

The big man spun the second chair around and sat down, his elbows on the upper back rung of the wooden chair. He leaned in. "But Reza, things change. For example, you claim you are loyal to the revolution, but the revolution was over some time ago. We are an established sovereign nation, a nation that contends with the largest and most powerful countries in the world. Those who are revolutionaries now are those who oppose us. Are you one of those, Reza? One who opposes the Islamic State of Iran?"

"No, Istad, never. I am a loyal citizen of the Islamic State. Have I not carried out twenty assassinations against the Islamic State's enemies? Did you tell the court I actually killed traitors who lived in the United States and were spies for the FBI? Did you tell them that? Did you tell them how I set up teams to bomb bookstores all over Europe for carrying blasphemous texts against Islam? Did you tell them how I have recruited many dissidents to supply us intelligence, thinking they were really opposing the regime and working for the counterrevolutionaries? Did you tell them these things?" His voice rose in pitch as he pleaded his case in one breath so the last words were almost squeaked as he ran out of air.

"Reza, it is true that you have been a useful operative, but the court cannot know these things for they are too secret. Only the top members of the Council of Ayatollahs know what it is we do for the State. We work only for them. Not even the minister knows fully what we do, for he is not to be anymore trusted than any other member of the elected government."

"But then, how can they know I am innocent? How can they know my value to the republic?" His sweat now was more condensation from the humidity in the small, closed room, but it still smelled of fear and urine. He sagged even more at the shoulders, but then a thought took hold, and he surged upward.

"The Americans! That's who it is! The Americans!" He believed he had found his deus ex machina. Allah had showed him the light. He could be saved. *"Allah be praised!* It is the Americans! Don't you see? *They* have set me up! They know your agent is a double, and they have passed on fabricated information!" This realization animated him. He still reeked of fear and urine, but the form of a rag doll draped on a chair had transfigured itself, once again, into the body of a man. He looked triumphantly up at his boss.

"Yes, Reza, it may be the Americans. We have given that some thought, but we are convinced they do not know our double agent continues to work for us. We have given them far too much good intelligence through him for them to suspect he is other than a valued agent. So, no, I don't really think it is the Americans. But in the end, what does it matter? They obviously have identified you, and your value to us as an overseas operative is over. And why would they spend a hundred thousand US dollars to set you up?"

The recently recaptured air escaped Reza's lungs, and his arms dropped to his side. He sat once again like a rag doll, limp with his legs splayed straight in front of him. "A hundred thousand dollars. There are bank accounts in my name with a hundred thousand dollars in them?" His head dropped on his chest, and he whispered, "Yes, a hundred thousand dollars is a lot of money."

His boss leaned forward, and producing two documents, ordered, "Sign these, they will allow us to recover our money from your accounts."

Reza took the offered pen and calmly did as he was told. "The Americans' money," he whispered silently. "The Americans' money."

The big man rose and drew himself up. "So, Reza, I have one more mission for you. We can no longer use you abroad, but now you must become an example to those who would oppose our Islamic State. And if you are truly innocent, Allah will know, and you will be received into paradise as a martyr. If not, then—" He turned and quickly left the room, leaving the door open, through which two guards entered. Taking Reza's arms, they lifted him from the chair. His legs did not work well, but it did not matter, for the gallows was just around the corner.

SAPPHIRES, SOVIET SPIES, AND SLINGSHOTS

1978, Southeast Asia

"FIND OUT WHY THIS SUPPOSEDLY covert officer was compromised, and then do something about it." Those were his orders from the deputy director for operations. Find out why a CIA officer assigned to a small Asian country had been compromised in the local press, stop the story from being picked up by the international press, and remedy whatever situation had caused the compromise. *And, oh—by the way—see if you can find the Holy Grail while you're at it,* he thought.

Damned little to go on, Jean mused as he settled in for the fourteen-hour flight to Bangkok. Closing his eyes, he reviewed what little he knew...

Although the "small Asian country" in question was not an obviously important player on the international scene, fears that its new government would continue to support the Soviet-sponsored Non-Aligned Movement's Indian Ocean Zone of

Peace (IOZP) were an issue of concern. IOZP was a potentially important treaty because it called for the removal of all foreign troops from the Indian Ocean and the creation of a nuclear-free zone. As such, it threatened the joint British-US base at Diego Garcia, which had been a major transshipment point for military supplies and was being eyed by the Department of Defense as a base for long-range interdiction capability in the Indian Ocean and Arabian Sea. Should the United States be booted from the Indian Ocean under the IOZP, Soviet ascendency in South Asia was likely, given the other recent geopolitical events in the area.

Was that it? he wondered. Could this compromise have had something to do with IOZP? *If so, how? And why?* Ah, well. He loved hard questions, and CIA was never at a loss...

Bangkok was as hot as he remembered it. Hot, humid, colorful Bangkok. Sex capital of the world. When he had served his Southeast Asian combat tour at Nakon Phanom—several hundred miles up-country—there had been only one city district in Bangkok where the brothels had been located. Now, the red-light district was enormous. But there were other attractions as well. Johnnie's Gems was a great place to purchase sapphires, and Raja's Tailors could do a hand-stitched suit in three days—two, if they really liked you.

He had roamed Thailand the first time with only a couple of pairs of khaki pants and some polo shirts in an overnight bag, but this time he had more luggage. He used one of his first in-town surveillance detection runs to stop at Raja's and have himself measured for a suit by none other than Raja himself. Interestingly, as his name suggested, Raja wasn't Thai but Sikh.

His family was part of the Sikh diaspora that had left India to seek business opportunities elsewhere, and Raja had become famous for his tailoring in Bangkok. Jean picked out some linen and some tightly woven Egyptian cotton and linen blends, and ordered three suits. He thought he might have need of them if he was going to spend any time operating in the Near East and South Asia. He also ordered some cotton dress shirts that were substantial enough to hold a slightly starched press even when sweated through. All in all, Raja's was a most pleasant experience.

The only piece of apparel he had purchased from Raja's during his previous visits to Bangkok—while flying combat-rescue and clandestine operations missions into North Vietnam, Laos, and Cambodia—had been an elephant-hide flying jacket that simply refused to wear out. He loved the jacket and wore it during his combat missions. Later, he had worn it each fall and spring—and sometimes in the winter with a sweater under it. It made him look…well, it made him look like someone who knew what he was doing, especially when he wore it with a pair of khakis, his Wellington boots, and his ubiquitous Ray-Ban Wayfarer sunglasses.

Johnnie's was another pleasant experience. He spent the better part of three hours in the store. He ordered a pair of two-carat yellow sapphire ear studs for his mother. While he was selecting those stones, a seven-carat rose sapphire captured his attention. It was pear-shaped and absolutely crying to be anchored to a gold chain as a pendant. His mother would never wear it, but he knew someone on whom it would look beautiful—although she might never wear it, for he might never have the occasion to give it to her, for she was another man's wife. Still, he bought the stone and made arrangements to have it set in twenty-one-carat gold as a pendant.

The shopping was much more productive than the meeting with the compromised CIA officer that followed at the conclusion of the surveillance detection run. The officer claimed to have no idea how his CIA affiliation had come to light or why he'd been exposed in the local press. To his listener, however, it appeared almost certain that one of the agents being handled by the officer, a midlevel officer in the Ministry of Foreign Affairs—code-named Tangible—had played a role.

Tangible was well-placed. He worked directly for the foreign minister, so it was easy to imagine he had been of interest to more than one intelligence service. If Tangible's CIA handler had failed to vet the agent adequately, it was very possible the CIA had not previously discovered that Tangible was a double agent. What didn't make sense was why—even if Tangible was working for the Soviets as well as the Americans—the Soviets would have considered the exposure of his handler, a minor CIA officer, to be of sufficient importance to risk the possibility of drawing attention to the case. Double agents were almost always run for the long term, so why was this compromise so important that it was worth jeopardizing the case? Just as the deputy director had asked, "Why now? Why him?" It appeared that finding the answer would have to begin with Tangible himself.

Jean wrote up his comments, offered some suggestions, and sent his message to Headquarters. The response was rapid. Jean was to temporarily replace the compromised officer and take over the Tangible case. An experienced surveillance team from Headquarters was dispatched to assist. It was their job to keep Tangible under surveillance after he left the operational meetings since both Jean and Headquarters thought that if Tangible was in fact a double agent, he would likely meet with his KGB handler as quickly as possible after the next meeting.

It took only two meetings before the team discovered Tangible hustling from his meeting with his new CIA officer to a meeting with a known KGB officer. The surveillance team took photos of the meeting and used a parabolic microphone to record the session. While the recording was not the best, it was sufficient to establish that Tangible was indeed a double agent, assigned by the KGB to report on his contacts with the CIA.

Jean now needed to know why the Soviets had risked Tangible to expose a low-level CIA officer. As he considered the puzzle, he grew more certain that this operation was, at base, about IOZP. According to information Tangible had been providing to the CIA, the new government strongly supported IOZP. But if this was the case, why was the KGB concerned?

Since the local journalist who had written the article exposing the CIA officer had not exposed Tangible, Jean assumed that the Soviets wanted to keep Tangible active. Very likely the information Tangible was providing to his CIA handler was inaccurate and intended to mislead. Jean smiled as he began to appreciate the increasing intricacy of the puzzle.

Jean was careful. He always used extensive surveillance detection routes before and after meeting Tangible, and he always made sure his routes terminated at the embassy. Since these were all late-evening meetings, it was unlikely there would be any embassy employees in the pay of the KGB who would be on duty and could identify him on his return. He had a good cover that allowed him to access the embassy at all hours, thus making his presence not an unusual occurrence. He took pains to make sure he went to the embassy during the evenings on days when he didn't have agent meetings to establish a pattern in the minds of any employees who might happen to be in the pay of another intelligence service.

His cover was that of a foreign buildings security adviser for the US Department of State, so he was able to meet with local and national law enforcement members to discuss security at the embassy and all the other US government sites in the country. This gave him entree to a number of high-ranking government officials, some of whom he began to cultivate as possible spies.

One of the most promising was the chief of the intelligence service. Having attended graduate school at the University of California–Santa Barbara, the general had fond memories of the United States and continued to travel there when his duties permitted. In his late fifties, he had an inordinate liking for Elvis Presley and Jim Reeves songs. It just happened that Jean, who played piano and had sung in college musicals, had more than a few Elvis and Jim Reeves songs in his repertory. He enjoyed playing and singing them almost as much as the general enjoyed hearing them. He coaxed the general to sing with him during a Christmas pantomime at the local gymkhana club, which had an old but serviceable piano in the members' lounge. After each practice session, he and the general would drink brandy and gingers—well, the general drank brandy and ginger ale; Jean just drank drams of brandy. They talked about local and international events, and the general became more expansive as the relationship grew. At the pantomime they sang a duet of "Blue Christmas," which both Elvis and Jim Reeves had recorded during their careers. The general's baritone resonated well with Jean's tenor, and they received a tremendous ovation from the crowd of mostly senior government officials, prominent businessmen, and their families.

It was after the party, early into the following morning, that the general—after downing his fifth brandy and ginger— asked if he could ask Jean a very sensitive question. Jean's "You can ask anything, but I may not answer" response drew a smile from the general, who then said, "Why do my government's overtures keep getting rebuffed by the United States?"

"I'm not following your question, General," Jean replied. "What overtures?"

The general explained how he, the president, and a group of center-right politicians wanted to speak about aligning their government with the interests of the Western powers but had to be very cautious, because those in the opposition in Parliament wanted to return political alignment to the Soviet Union as it had been under the former Socialist government. He noted that the president had directed their ambassador in Washington to reach out secretly to members of the US Department of State to determine whether the United States was prepared to seriously entertain a negotiation on the proposition.

Jean knew nothing of any such approach, but then he didn't find this surprising because the Department of State never, but never, allowed CIA officers to meddle. The State Department was always prepared to take the intelligence the CIA provided but never allowed CIA operations officers to become involved in the actual conduct of diplomacy. Such conduct would be anathema to State Department officers who, Jean believed, saw themselves as members of the intellectual elite and, as such, the closest thing to an aristocracy in the United States.

Still, truth be known, CIA officers had much more impact on the actual conduct of foreign policy than many State Department officers. Some ambassadors and senior State officers understood the tremendous advantage of using previously established secret contacts within a government to plant information that could result in favorable negotiations. More important, they used CIA-provided intelligence on the tactics and positions the foreign government planned to adopt in negotiations. That some ambassadors spent more time behind closed doors with their CIA station chiefs and analysts than with their embassy staff did not go unnoticed by even semiastute observers.

Still, Jean would not have been briefed on any diplomatic approaches, and he told the general as much. He did promise to check as soon as the holidays were over and Washington returned to its normal chaotic schedule.

On Christmas morning, Jean sat on the balcony of the seaside apartment he had rented. He had eschewed embassy housing because it was in an American compound, and the last thing he had wanted was to arouse the interest of embassy wives playing "spot the spook." Compounds were one of the worst aspects of living abroad under US government cover. Often you didn't have a choice because embassy housing boards assigned housing to permanent party personnel, but since Jean was acting in a temporary duty capacity under separate orders he could expense his apartment as an operational necessity and thus avoid the tedious existence of compound living.

As he contemplated the sunrise over the water, he thought about the general's question. He had already sent an eyes-only cable directly to the division chief, asking about secret entreaties from the country's ambassador. Given that the ambassador would have had to communicate through the foreign ministry, it seemed likely that the Soviet double agent—and therefore the Soviets—knew that the president was secretly seeking to realign his country's interests with those of the Western powers. Had the discrediting of the CIA officer been part of an attempt to scuttle that initiative and any subsequent negotiations it might precipitate? But there were no negotiations. In fact, according to the general, the United States had repeatedly rebuffed the secret entreaties. So why mount an operation to discredit US personnel?

Then Jean had one of those "A-ha!" moments that come so seldom, but when they do, everything becomes clear. The US had never been asked. The ambassador in Washington was either in the pay of the Soviets or acting on behalf of the out-of-power local Socialist party. Given the operation against the CIA officer, it was probably the former. The ambassador had never approached the State Department with the president's request.

The Soviets, recognizing in advance that sooner or later the inquiring President would seek another venue for approaching the United States—if only to ask why his government was being ignored—had engineered the exposure of the CIA officer to lay groundwork for responding to that eventuality. If the United States had already been discredited by planted stories about CIA activities in the country, the president would be playing into the hands of the opposition if he attempted to open talks with the United States.

It all fit, and it was all about IOZP. Tangible, the "rebuffed" entreaties, the exposed CIA officer…In solving the puzzle, Jean had identified two Soviet spies and a dedicated Soviet active measures effort. Now what?

He didn't want to put anything into official electronic traffic yet, opting instead for a handwritten letter to the deputy director explaining exactly what was happening and what he thought should be done. Using the secret writing ink he had been issued, Jean wrote out a detailed invisible message, carefully following prescribed procedures to avoid detection. Once the secret ink had dried, he wrote a "real" letter on top of the invisible one, complaining about the conditions in the country and Washington's failure to provide him with a permanent assignment. It was exactly the type of letter an officer whining about his career would write to a boss. It was titillating enough to satisfy even the most aggressive counterespionage agent who, should the letter be subjected to closer scrutiny, would not be looking for invisible ink, but for hidden meanings in the visible letter's words.

Jean dispatched the letter in the personal care of a State Department officer who was leaving post the day after Christmas to return to the United States for some personal leave. The letter carried an internal State Department address on the outer envelope. Once received by that office, the inside letter would be removed and forwarded to the appropriate address at Langley. Jean enjoyed the rest of the holiday season in the mountains, having been invited to a hill station for the New Year by some local business contacts he had made. He sang, played piano, and danced with the wives, daughters, and mistresses of the wealthy, knowing there would be some type of response waiting when he returned to town.

After a pleasant, if slightly uneasy, holiday Jean returned to find a response waiting for him—an "eyes-only" cable from the deputy director for operations himself. It was brief, saying only that a trusted individual was being dispatched by the White House to conduct the necessary negotiations and that this individual had the authority of the US president to agree to certain provisions that would be contained within the US offer. Jean would make himself available to that person and act as his assistant, but only in private. Jean was not to attend any public events or, for that matter, private negotiations with the government. He was, however, to review everything with the representative and offer both information and advice as needed. The envoy was not a member of the State Department but rather a special envoy with extensive experience in diplomatic negotiations.

Jean knew that he would also have to suggest some manner to remove the Soviet agents from the country. So when the special envoy arrived—not, of course, as a special envoy but as a friend of the ambassador making a personal visit—Jean proposed sweetening the deal by offering to present proof of the work of Soviet agents to undermine the current administration's efforts. And to that end the envoy presented the president with photos and the recording of Tangible meeting with his KGB handler. The envoy also told the president that no attempt to open negotiations with the US government had been made by his ambassador. In fact, the last time anyone in the State Department had spoken with his ambassador was six months previously, and the subject had been a request for a US Navy ship visit to one of the ports in the country. At that time the ambassador had cautioned against asking for such ship visits because the current government was staunchly in the Non-Aligned camp and would never consider allowing a US warship in any of their harbors.

With that opening it took little time to conclude the negotiations and, within a month, a large US warship was scheduled to visit not just any port, but the capital's port a few miles up the coast. The country's ambassador had been quietly recalled from Washington to be replaced by the president's nephew, and Tangible had been reassigned within the ministry to a position in the office of consular affairs where he was responsible for answering complaints by citizens abroad about what they believed were failures of their local embassies to support them.

The KGB officer meeting with Tangible had been asked to leave the country along with two of his colleagues. Jean had thrown the names of the two other KGB officers into the mix at the last minute. True, they had not, to his knowledge, been involved in the case, but the local government didn't know that, and there had to be some sort of payback for the outing of the CIA officer, regardless of how incompetent that officer might have been.

Based on a suggestion from the president's office, the local journalist who had outed the CIA officer was assigned to Moscow as a foreign correspondent. This, by his publisher, after the president had spoken with that publisher about truthfulness in reporting—strongly suggesting that the journalist had fabricated the CIA story, and as such, there needed to be a retraction. The publisher himself penned the story of an overzealous reporter not checking his sources. He offered apologies to the United States and its diplomatic personnel. Strangely, or perhaps not, little of the journalist's reporting during his Moscow sojourn would make it into the paper.

The president announced that after careful consideration, his government had decided the IOZP was not a treaty in the interests of the smaller nations in the region and that his country would no longer advocate United Nations adoption of that treaty.

Shortly thereafter it was announced that the country had negotiated for part of the importation quota of woolen and cotton garments into the United States, opening a major market for the new garment factories being constructed in the country, some with loans from US banks and others from Western European banks. There was not a single factory sponsored by a Soviet or Warsaw Pact country.

It was a good piece of work for Jean. In his first time at bat in the majors he had hit a home run. He was proud of what he had accomplished. Yet when he remembered the assignment, it was more for what he hadn't written in his final report than what he had. True, the Soviets had paid a three-to-one price in operations officers lost, but Jean wanted something to really prick their balloon.

He had come to realize after several months in the country that one of the hardest items to acquire was a windshield for a car. Because all cars and spare parts were imported, the tariffs and import laws left over from the previous Socialist government meant it took months to import just one item. So at one o'clock on the morning he was to leave the country, Jean took his combat slingshot and a bag of steel ball bearings and embarked on an operation he had planned for some time.

Just outside the wall of the Soviet embassy was a car park where all the embassy and KGB operational vehicles were kept. These cars weren't Russian Ladas but locally rented vehicles provided by a company owned by a Socialist member of parliament. They were all nicely lined up in orderly rows under the watch of two local guards.

Using part of a stick of incense folded inside the cover of a matchbook as a time delay fuse, Jean dropped it in a large pile of trash and debris around the corner from the car park. He then climbed into the branches of a large tree across the narrow alley from the car park and waited for the guards to respond to the fire. Then it was one windshield after another until he ran out of ball bearings. He hit each windshield on the driver's side causing a spider web of cracks that would make it impossible to drive the cars at night and dangerous during the day. It surprised him when one of the windshields actually broke and pieces of glass fell into the car. Then he took a folded paper airplane from his bag and launched it out over the car park. On the paper he had printed, "Down with the tyranny of the oligarchs, long live the Revolution!" It was signed, "The People's Party for True Equality."

The piece of paper he used for the airplane had come from the trash of the Novosti office that provided cover for several KGB officers. It had been picked out of the trash by one of the minor agents Jean had recruited during his assignment. These agents were beggars, street vendors, and other types who could go unnoticed or remarked upon by potential targets he wanted to keep an eye on. In this case the paper would probably have the fingerprints of several Russians on it. Jean wore latex gloves when handling the paper just as he would when creating a secret writing message. He had wiped each ball bearing before putting it in his bag so any fingerprint testing would show only prints from whatever Russians had handled the balls and the paper, plus those of Jean's agent. But, of course, there would be no record of the agent's prints, so those would be listed as unidentified. Let them try to figure out what Russian officials were doing with their prints on a letter from an anti–Soviet Union communist group.

Out of the tree and back to his apartment. He had just enough time to shower and change before the car picked him up to take him to the airport for the early morning flight back to Europe and then onward to the States. On the way to the airport, he stopped by the chief of station's home, rousting him out of bed to ask that he put a box in the diplomatic pouch. Inside the box was Jean's slingshot. He was sorry he had not been able to stay around to see how the Soviets reacted. He realized this was a very minor coup de main, but it was a long war and you took your victories when and where you could find them.

At the airport, he processed through emigration and went into the small lounge to wait to board the bus that would take him to the airplane. As he looked for a seat, the general appeared. He took Jean by the arm, escorting him into the VIP waiting area. As they entered, Jean noted some people being escorted out of the area by uniformed guards he suspected were part of the general's retinue.

"Jean," the general began. "I suspect you are more than you claim to be, but whatever and whoever you are, please know we welcome your help." He handed Jean an oblong presentation case covered in blue damask. "With the thanks of our president and our people." Inside was a largish medal of a lion rampant standing on a golden banner. Both lion and banner were surrounded by an alternating blue and yellow sapphire encrusted oval. On the scroll was embossed in French: "Pour le Merit." The medal was heavy, and there was no question it was high-grade gold. It hung from a silk ribbon of white, gold, and maroon. Engraved on the reverse was "Presented to a Friend for Valorous Service."

"I would place this around your neck, but I think you would probably prefer I just shake your hand," the general said, holding out his hand.

As Jean took his hand he looked hard at the general. He knew the emotion was sincere, and that sincerity had a great impact on him. He had not expected this encounter, thinking he would slip away little noticed. Now he needed the right words, but just as he had decided how to respond, one of the general's aides arrived in a hurry, whispering something to the general that seemed to amuse him.

"Jean, I had intended to stay and see you off, but it appears our Russian friends have a great problem. Their ambassador believes they are under attack from a reactionary group of terrorists." He stepped back, saluted Jean, and turned to leave; but as he did so, he turned back and asked, "You wouldn't know anything about this group of reactionaries would you?"

Jean smiled as he replied, "General, were I to give you my word I have no knowledge of any group aspiring to undo the Soviet Union I would be lying, and I would prefer not to lie to a friend."

The general also smiled, and as he once again turned to leave, he said, "I thought as much. A long and safe life, my friend."

THE TOWERS OF BABEL HAVE FALLEN

September 11, 2001, Jeddah, Saudi Arabia

"TADMIR ALNIZAM AL'AMRIKI!" ECHOED THROUGH the room. "Destroy the American system! Allahu Akbar! Allahu Akbar! God is great! God is great!"

"Allah will confound the infidels! This is a great day!"

Abdullah was beside himself. He had never been so proud. Allah's holy warriors had triumphed over the great Shaitan. Soon Allah's peace would rule the world, just as Muhammad had predicted. He watched CNN with the others, crowded into the room above the Chicken Broast in the Bani Malik section of Jeddah. He was so excited he almost lost control of his bladder. Drops of urine stained the cotton pants under his thobe.

His was the secret that the burning towers were the work of his holy brothers. All Saudis. He wondered if the time was right. He could announce it here. He could establish his credibility and recruit others to the cause. They would rally to him in great numbers.

No, he thought. *There may be a Mubahith spy in the room. But aren't there even members of the movement in that dreaded secret police? Just as there are members in the royal family. Still, it would not do to lose myself at so great a moment.*

He looked again at the television. One of the towers had begun to fall. It created a haboob of debris billowing down the street toward the cameraman, who began to run, tripping as he tried to record the destruction and escape it at the same time. Another electric thrill went through Abdullah. The plan was working perfectly. The towers were collapsing. He stood there, agape. The cheering had stopped. Everyone was transfixed by the collapse. Then all at once, as in chorus, "Allahu Akbar!" rang through the room. "Allhamdulilai! Allhamdulilai! Thanks to Allah! Thanks to Allah! Allahu Akbar!"

Abdullah now thought of Mahmud. He must see Mahmud for instructions. Still, he must be careful, for now even the Mutawi, as well as the Mukhabarat and the Mubahith, would be seeking dissidents to question about what they knew of this wonderful coup. The religious police were everywhere. He did not worry as much about Mukhabarat, the intelligence service, for they were more outwardly oriented. And had he not just recently heard the rumor that its head was a member of the Muslim Brotherhood? Yet, the Brotherhood might object to this operation, since it would bring down the wrath of America on the Muslim world, thus interfering in the Brotherhood's long-term plans to establish dominance. But perhaps the Brotherhood was a part of this. Abdullah did not know.

The wrath of America. That was what they wanted: to create a hatred in America for the Muslim world. A conflagration was needed. American forces in the Middle East, killing Muslims. That was Sharif Usama bin Ladin's goal. Now it would come. They had not failed this time. Now there was more work to be done. Abdullah must see Mahmud immediately.

October 2001, on the escarpment, Taif, Saudi Arabia

"Mahmud, why do we not have another large scale operation ready to go?" Abdullah was frustrated. It had been over a month since the towers had been destroyed. It had been an even better operation than planned. No one expected other buildings to collapse as well. America was devastated. The world was shocked. Advantage lay in the arms of Allah's holy warriors, and Abdullah chafed they were not pursuing that advantage. "Why must we wait for the Americans to respond? What if they don't respond? What if they don't send their army?" Abdullah's concern was evident as his voice rose in pitch with each question.

"Abdullah, calm yourself." Mahmud sternly addressed his younger protégé. "You know I lived in America. I know them. They are like a camel, lazy unless you beat them with a stick. They spit and bite, but put the slightest burr under the saddle blanket, and they go crazy. Verily, we placed not a burr but an entire acacia tree under their blanket. They cannot help but react. Listen to their President Bush on CNN. He has declared a war upon us. A war! Ha! He does not know what war is. We will send his soldiers home in boxes, or without their arms, legs, and eyes. He will wish he had never heard of Islam or Allah's holy warriors. We will drive him ahead of us as a wolf drives sheep." Mahmud's voice also rose as he gesticulated during his proclamation.

The others in the room were transfixed by his baritone voice and by his ebony eyes, which shone from below the brow made by the agal holding down his ghutra. He wore white, the color of a sharif, like Sharif Usama.

Others arrived; by twos and threes they came, so as to avoid watchers who might wonder at a gathering so large. Among them were new recruits from the university. Unroyal Saudis, second-class citizens in a world increasingly populated and controlled by royals, they found personal worth in the status of holy warrior.

Mahmud spoke of how Sharif Usama awaited America's army in Afghanistan. How he would inflict terrible retribution upon them with his Taliban allies. The mountains were theirs. The Persians, British, and Russians had not been able to subjugate the mountain tribes, so what hubris made the Americans think they could do it? The mountains of Afghanistan would become the killing fields for the death of the American empire. "Kill the Americans!" Mahmud shouted at the finish. He then impressed on each one present the need for secrecy. For although many in the royal family supported the cause of the Wahabi, there were those who toadied to the infidels in order to tighten their own grasp on power. He cautioned carefulness when speaking with others, because the university and all the ministries were infested with the rodents of the secret police.

Still, he reminded them, the martyrs of September 11 had preceded them as students. Soon, he promised, there would be an army of holy warriors that would sweep across Arabia and into the rest of the world, praising Allah and pressing the infidels in front of it, imposing the will of Allah on the unclean and purifying the cities of the world with Shariah. All would submit to Allah and they, the unroyals, would be in charge.

After all had left, two or three at a time, Abdullah asked Mahmud, "Is Sharif Usama safe? We should not want to lose him in battle with the Americans."

"He is deep in a cave near Tora Bora," Mahmud told him. "And in an emergency our friends in the intelligence service of Pakistan have offered him safe passage and a hideaway."

"But he cannot hide now," Abdullah protested. "We have the Americans where we want them. World opinion will turn in our favor when they start killing civilians with their bombs, as they did in Iraq when they drove Saddam from Kuwait. We must have another strike now. Another thrust at the heart of the American system!" Abdullah's voice rose again. When he became very excited, he sounded like a woman.

"Take hold of yourself, Abdullah. Everything is as it should be. I know the Americans. I lived there many years. I went to Harvard College. We already have the American college students. All we do is show a picture of a poor Palestinian and a Jewish soldier, and the American students cry for justice. The faculties, too, are on our side. That is more because it is the contrarian position to take, and American academics believe they exercise power through contrarianism. It is strange, but it is true. One wonders how they would govern should their contrarianism ever gain them political positions of authority. They would have to be against themselves." Mahmud laughed.

"It is simple psychology, Abdullah, simple psychology. The Americans are a simple people, easily swayed, and quick to anger."

"Yes, I see." Abdullah didn't, but he did not want to appear unintelligent. Mahmud had, indeed, lived in America for many years. He had even become a citizen. He claimed to know others, living there still, who would recruit and help further the goals of the holy warriors of Islam. Still, there were other things Abdullah wished to learn. Some were questions posed to him by potential recruits at the university. He sought Mahmud's guidance.

"Mahmud, when speaking with those who wish to know more about becoming a holy warrior, I am sometimes asked why the reward for a martyr is virgins. They ask because they believe sex with a virgin is painful for both. And they worry about the blood, and whether there is actual pleasure in the deflowering of a virgin. Most are inexperienced in sex and ask from ignorance. How shall I respond to them?"

"Abdullah, you are a good recruiter, but you have much to learn. To possess a virgin is the ultimate in demonstrating a man's authority. It isn't about the pleasure of sex, but the pleasure of power. Allah made women to serve men. The Quran 2:223 tells us, 'Women are your fields: go, then, into your fields whence you please.' And it tells us in 4:34, 'Men have authority over women because God has made the one superior to the other, and because they spend their wealth to maintain them. Good women are obedient. They guard their unseen parts because God has guarded them. As for those from whom you fear disobedience, admonish them and forsake them in beds apart, and beat them.'"

Mahmud was an expert at quoting the Quran. He reached now for the carafe and poured himself another glass of sweet mint tea. Kicking his sandals from his feet, he leaned back against the overstuffed Italianate sofa. Taking off his kufia, he scratched the balding pate underneath. He sipped the tea. He wished for something stronger, but that would have to wait for later. Now he needed to educate Abdullah further.

"Abdullah, it is time I taught you about the exercise of power. Since you, like Ali and Fouad, are my protégé, and you may have to represent me at times, you need to learn these things. I do not expect you to learn this all at once, but it is important you understand the concepts." Mahmud turned so that his legs and feet were now on the sofa. He settled his back against the large bolstered arm.

"There are those above us who want to control not just the Middle East but larger segments of the world. They are the Brotherhood. Now, the Brotherhood includes princes, ministers, bankers, and investment brokers in the kingdom, the emirates, and Switzerland. There are members in England, France, Germany, Turkey, Malaysia, Indonesia, and other countries throughout the world. There are even groups in America that represent the Brotherhood. There are politicians and generals from a number of these countries who are members, as well as many who are not but are paid by the Brotherhood to do their bidding. As you know, there are many intelligence officers, especially in Pakistan—and not a few in the kingdom—who belong as well. These are the people who exercise authority. They have money and position to make things happen, but they must remain hidden, or they might lose that money and position. That's where you and I come in. We are the next level of the Brotherhood. We make things happen. We recruit warriors to the cause, and we represent the Brotherhood to the leadership of other Islamic groups who wish to establish a caliphate." Mahmud again scratched the itch at the top of his head. He wasn't sure why he itched so. He wondered if it had to do with the new hair restorative he was using.

He continued to lecture Abdullah. "When the Islamic army sweeps across the Middle East, you and I will have our reward here on earth. I want no more than to be a regional suzerain. It is the least of what I deserve. Then we shall have all the virgins we want. And anything else for that matter. Then, after a long life, we will join Allah and Muhammad for our heavenly reward for advancing the cause of Islam. It is too easy Abdullah. We are the smart ones. Like the hidden ones, we do not have to suffer the physical trauma of dying for the faith, but we shall profit from those who do. Religion is a tool of power. Yes, Abdullah, you have much to learn about the exercise of power."

March 2002, an apartment on the Pelikanstrasse, Bern, Switzerland

"Mahmud, the Brotherhood is concerned about the lack of American military response to the attacks on the towers and the Pentagon." The speaker wore a thousand-dollar Armani suit and was smoking a small dark cigarillo. On the table next to his chair sat a glass containing twenty-four-year-old scotch. He had the look of a banker, which was just as well, since he was one. He continued, "You promised us that the Americans would respond to the destruction of the twin towers with another major military buildup in Saudi Arabia that we could use for propaganda purposes. Also, we have clients who are heavily invested in American armament industries. If there is no buildup, then there are no additional expenditures from which we profit. Without that profit our ability to support worldwide jihad is lessened." He drew on the cigarillo, inhaled the smoke, and then blew it upward toward the ceiling.

"Now we have the American president declaring a national security imperative on energy self-sufficiency. He is issuing executive orders for a pipeline from Canada to the American gulf to bring oil not just from Canada, but new fields in North Dakota and South Dakota. He is crafting a program to build new refineries near the Canadian border, in Washington State, and in North Dakota to refine the oil nearer the production points. He is overriding the conservationists' objections through the imposition of this national security imperative to allow this new oil drilling technique called fracking. He proposes to pay for these facilities through the use of national defense energy bonds available only to American citizens. Do you have any idea how negatively this will affect the Brotherhood if he is successful?" He sipped at the scotch, but he had not finished.

"More than that, if this president succeeds he will make the United States a supplier of energy, which will drop prices in the United States, making it cheaper for manufacturers to pay higher wages, and we will begin to see the overseas manufacturing facilities returning to the United States. We are too heavily invested in the cheap labor markets to sustain such a change." He drew again deeply on the cigarillo.

Mahmud had quietly listened. He knew why he had been called to Switzerland, and he was prepared.

"Eyewash. Pure eyewash. You are a man of the world, a successful banker, and a manipulator of no small prowess. Surely you see this for what it is. The American president is afraid to fight us. He is making political moves in an attempt to consolidate power. He will not succeed. Already the right is calling him a coward, and the left continues to press him on the issue of women in Islam and other human rights matters. The oil companies will pay their congressmen and senators to block his attempts at this energy program. You may be reading the wrong newspapers, or watching CNN with too jaundiced an eye. The politicians will never allow these things to happen. It threatens their sinecures. Certainly the *Washington Post* and the *New York Times* cannot be supporting such an approach."

He stopped a moment and then said, "I recommend you read papers like the *Harvard Crimson*. It will show you where the American students are. We have done well in seeding anti-Israeli sentiment among the students in American colleges. Although I admit, it doesn't take much, given the way the Israeli government is acting." Mahmud knew he was talking to someone with even more experience with the Americans than he, but still, Mahmud had studied political science at Harvard and was an American citizen.

After a moment's silence, he played what he knew would be his trump card. "What the Americans cannot control is Islam. We will always be able to call the faithful to jihad. Eventually they will have to fight and, when they do, they will fall into our trap. Although we tore the towers down in less than a day, it took years to put the plan in place. Have patience. We will succeed."

September 2002, a house in Sa'dah, North of Yemen

"Salam Allekum," Mahmud welcomed his Yemeni brothers in the manner of all Arabs, and his Afghan and Somali brothers in the manner of all Muslims. Coffee, heavy with cardamom, was offered and taken. The watchers from the streets checked in to assure the house did not seem to be under surveillance. The overnight trip through the desert from Najran, in the South of Saudi, had taken longer than anticipated. Mahmud was tired. Moreover, he was angry. Angry at having his judgment questioned by those of lesser perspective. Angry at the Americans for their lack of response. Angry at the press for not doing more to prick the American president and Congress. Now this duma was called, not by him, but by the Afghans. They wanted questions answered. They no longer hosted Sharif Usama. He had fled to the comfort of a villa in Pakistan. They seldom heard from him. He might as well be in an American prison. Couriers with promised money and weapons had not arrived. Where, they asked, was the influx of holy warriors promised by Mahmud, Zarwahiri, and the sheik himself?

There were similar problems in Yemen and Somalia. Couriers dispatched with messages and money had disappeared. Somewhere something was wrong. This was not what had been promised them. The Somalis started to take ships for the ransom, but now their own boats were disappearing in the Gulf of Aden and their sailors never heard from afterward.

It was the Afghan Taliban who began. "Mahmud, where are the Americans? We have been ready for them an entire year. Our fighters begin to talk of going home. We tell them Allah will produce the enemy, but the enemy never comes. We see tiny aircraft sometimes, but it is not like the Russians. No helicopters, no soldiers. Where are they? We are losing our commanders. They use the satellite telephones you provided, and then a missile comes, seemingly from nowhere. We cannot use these telephones. Now we are dependent, as in our fathers' time, on using couriers, and even some of them disappear. We have had no word from our Pakistani intelligence contacts in months. We sent two representatives to meet with them, and neither came back. When we sent two more to seek out the commanders sent before them, only one returned. He had watched from a distance as his cousin was arrested by troops at the gate of the intelligence service's headquarters. Something is wrong. We think it is the Americans. They are not sending soldiers; they are sending spies and saboteurs. They are pressuring not just our governments, but individuals as well. They are making a secret war on us. This is not what we expected.

"I heard from a brother, just back from Iraq, that someone is arming the Kurds, and they are fighting our Islamic brothers in the north. And today we hear on Radio Moscow and on the BBC that America has made a proposition to the United Nations that Afghanistan should be divided into five separate states based on tribal identity. They are even suggesting that Waziristan be taken from Pakistan and made part of a state of Pashtunastan. The tribes of the north, south, and west are going to like the idea. The Tajiks, Uzbeks, and Turkmens have wanted always to occupy parts of the land, and this proposal would make the areas where their tribal languages constitute the majority into protectorates of Tajikistan, Uzbekistan, and Turkmenistan. The western part would fall under the Shia of Iran for protection. It will defeat our plan to dominate the country and impose Sharia law. It will lessen our forces and create new enemies for us. Already we suspect those we thought allies in the north and west are preparing to declare their own states. Even our own Pashtuns are liking the idea of a Pashtunastan."

As he had done with the banker, Mahmud assured his brothers that Islam would prevail, and that in prevailing they would gain and retain power. Still, in his heart, there was a growing fear the Americans were somehow doing something he had not predicted. He needed to study this more closely. Americans always had to stand toe to toe with their adversaries to prove they were the better man. American leaders had to beat their chests in public to proclaim their accomplishments. What seemed to be happening was so un-American. Next week he would again meet his American contacts. He would seek more information on this phenomenon. They would know how to counter it.

"I bid you not to go in peace, but to leave angrier than ever at the Americans for refusing to act like men." He dismissed the duma.

October 2002, a house on the eastern edge of Dali, Cyprus

"I'm afraid we bear bad news." The speaker was a tall, thin man with olive skin and a prominent nose. He wore a khaki safari jacket over blue jeans. He looked Egyptian, but he spoke with the accent of a Manhattan native.

"We learned this morning the American president, or someone working for him, has convinced three imams to come together to issue a fatwa against the killing of innocents, even in jihad. Our informants in Washington tell us they have a Somali imam from Washington, DC, a Syrian imam from Dearborn, Michigan, and an Iraqi imam from Brooklyn."

Mahmud sat forward in his chair. He asked, "How did you learn this information this morning?"

The tall man replied, "I spoke with one of my clients in Washington. He is well placed to learn these things from contacts he has within various government departments. There are, you know, many in places like the State Department who support the cause of Palestinian self-determination and see our struggle as part of pushing the Israelis from the Holy Land. He will report when he discovers more information about who the imams are and when the fatwa is to be issued."

Mahmud drew his hand across his face in exasperation. "Do you not understand that the Americans listen to phone calls?"

The man waved the back of his hand at Mahmud. "I'm an American citizen. They are not allowed to listen in on my calls. Besides, since I am a lawyer, I carry my Washington sources as clients, so the NSA and FBI are doubly prohibited from listening in on my calls."

Mahmud could only shake his head. He knew there were pragmatists somewhere in even the weakest of administrations who would find a way around that prohibition. He was torn, wanting to know more about the imams and their fatwa, but not wanting his American contact to speak with anyone on the phone. Still it might be the only way he would learn enough to take action against these traitors.

Emphatically Mahmud said, "We must discredit these imams. We will have our own people issue a fatwa calling for the death of these apostates."

The tall man looked perplexed, "But isn't that playing right into the hands of the American government? Such a fatwa will split Sunni Islam into two divisions: those in favor of the killing of innocents and those opposed. You will be at war with yourselves. Isn't it bad enough that you Sunni are at war with the Shia? A further rift in the religion can only do harm to your cause."

Mahmud was becoming more and more exasperated. This is not what he had expected of the meeting. He tried to pay attention for the remainder, but he had become obsessed with the fact his contact was using the telephone to discuss important matters. His self-preservation instincts had been triggered, and he decided to cut the meeting short. He exhorted the tall man not to discuss matters except in face-to-face meetings, and before he left, went to the windows on all sides of the house to look for the possibility the Americans had followed this contact to the meeting. He saw nothing and, relieved, left in the rental car he had hired at the airport in Larnaca. He would travel on to Nicosia where he planned to meet with a new contact from Jordan. The contact promised to help establish a jihadi movement in Gaza. It was a significant opportunity.

As he checked into the Hilton in Nicosia, Mahmud was prepared to do what he always did. He would turn down the first room they offered him and ask for something on the ground floor. However, this time the Hilton gave him a room on the ground floor. He did not think it strange since he knew hotel chains were now keeping profiles on frequent customers. Still, he found it just a little unsettling. He would have to change hotels in the future.

He would be meeting his Jordanian contact in the old city near the Turkish border. The Jordanian had suggested the site because if something untoward happened, they could quickly cross the border into Turkey and into the arms of—if not supportive, at least understanding—Muslims.

Mahmud found the house without trouble. He looked for the safety signal of a flowerpot placed in the front window. It was there, so his contact was inside, and all was ready for the meeting. He was sure the contact would be surreptitiously watching from an upper window to ensure Mahmud had not been followed. Closing the door as he entered intensified the darkness of the hallway. There was light in the back of the house and he slowly moved toward it, feeling his way as his eyes sought to adjust to the darkness. The prick felt like the sting of a wasp. He swatted at his neck to kill the insect.

November 2002, a house on Sharia Libya, Jeddah, Saudi Arabia

Abdullah, Fouad, and Ali waited.

Ali was the first to mention the fatwa, noting how, at his university, there was considerable questioning of the loss of the right to heaven and the concept of martyrdom. Fouad echoed his concerns but had even more distressing news. There was a rumor circulating that the body of a member of the Brotherhood had been discovered buried with the head of a pig. Now it was being said that the Americans would bury the bodies of martyrs with parts of a pig, making them unclean and thus unable to enter heaven.

Abdullah tried to calm the others, but he, too, had heard the rumor. The number of those attending his meetings to discuss jihad and support the cause had grown smaller and smaller. Abdullah knew the power of rumor in the Arab world. Mahmud had told him the story of the Libyan attack on the Qaba' in 1979. The rumor that the Americans were responsible had spread quickly through the Muslim world, and two American embassies were sacked and burned. Worse, perhaps there was truth in this rumor. The Americans were acting differently than before. Mahmud would know how to handle this.

So, Abdullah, Fouad, and Ali waited...

October 2014, a house on Black Oak Ridge, Tennessee

The man closed the book and put it on the table. He sighed. "It's a shame. Such a shame this ended up written as fiction, and not as the actual history of how things could have been, if only the politicians and the generals had considered alternatives to pressing a war so they could beat their chests and trumpet their triumphs. So many deaths, so much money. God save us from the idealists, the media, and the politicians. It's a shame. A real shame."

A Party at the
Diplomatic Club
(A Night to Remember)

HE PULLED THE PASTEL CRAYON toward him to give the drawn ceramic pot a stroke of umber. He feathered it with his tissue. Then another stroke, this time outward. It needed to be darker. There had been a small palm tree. How to draw a palm tree? He stopped and stepped back from the easel. Too much detail or not enough? It was supposed to be only a suggestive sketch. A sketch that would recall the wet warmth of the night and capture the heaviness of the smoke that swirled beneath the electric ceiling fans. Fans rusted from years of humidity and neglect. Fans that creaked as they turned, adding their complaints to a room full of people who complained about the third-world outpost they now called home.

And outpost it was. It had little to offer the world in the way of resources—no oil, no gold, no diamonds, no uranium. Just lots of people. People and illness, people and hunger, people and poverty. In this capital city, there was not a single elevator that worked, although there was at least one twenty-story building. What meat there was, was sold in open markets where, to see the meat itself, you had to hit the carcass with a stick to dislodge the flies that had settled to lay their eggs.

The telephone system did not work, so foreign diplomats and aid workers carried small radios to communicate with each other. Bicycle messengers were used to conduct conversations with businessmen or government officials. Your bicycle messenger would deliver your message and wait for a response. He would then bring that response to you. Often as not, the response was another question to which you had to send an answer. It could take the better part of a day (and sometimes more) to handle an issue that, with a working telephone system, would have taken no more than ten minutes even if you engaged in the formal pleasantries the local culture demanded be the commencement of all conversations.

So why, then, be there? That was a question many people— especially the relatives of some of the diplomatic representatives— asked. But what they often missed in their initial assessments was that while this country was not rich in natural resources and had more problems than could ever truly be solved, it enjoyed a natural harbor and direct geographic access to many of the world's major oil tanker routes. In the event of war between the Soviet Union and the West, it could be used as a base either to interdict or to protect the tankers making their way from oil-rich countries to the West or even the Far East. Thus, it was necessary to send the brightest of intelligence officers there to play the great game of spy versus spy, intrigue versus counterintrigue, each side trying to gain an upper hand with the corrupt government full of officials with Swiss bank accounts, ready to flee the country at the first hint of trouble. Each senior government official was like a playing card, and the foreign players attempted to collect as many cards in their hands as they could. It would be interesting when it came time to lay the cards on the table, because some government ministers existed as knaves in the hand of more than one intelligence officer.

He remembered all of this as he drew the palm. It was easier than he thought. Some brown with black spots for the short trunk, then a flick of the wrist with some leaf-green pastel for the fronds. It was better than he had thought he could do when he started the drawing. Some white, then very light strokes of gray, feathered again with a tissue, created the smokiness that suffused the large room.

It had been smoky and wet, but he was not aware of any drawing technique that could re-create the dampness of the room. Neither could he depict in a drawing the swirling eddies of smoke under the slowly turning ceiling fans. Once again he stepped back and looked at his work. *Refrigerator art,* he thought. *Not good enough for the wall but maybe something for the door of the refrigerator. It is, after all, the thought that counts, isn't it?* He asked himself whether she would remember it the same way he had. *Did it mean the same to her?*

The KGB colonel had done little to maintain his cover as a trade delegate. He openly intimated to some that he was not *just* KGB, but that he was a very senior officer. He did this in an effort to intimidate. He was successful with some, less so with others. That night he had tried to intimidate the younger

American officer who—an experienced combat veteran himself, and an accomplished card player in the great game—was having none of it.

He smiled as he looked at the picture. Should he attempt to draw people, perhaps only as silhouettes? The two of them standing at the bar? No, he was not skilled enough for that. The room would have to do. It wasn't bad. His smile became broader as he thought of the prose he had written for the card. He was a better poet than artist, although he could claim no fame in either discipline. Once again he was buoyed by the old adage, "It's the thought that counts."

She sat across the table from him at the little restaurant that had become "their place." It was always crowded, and the food was good. The waiters knew them by name, as did some of the other regular patrons.

First, he gave her the now-framed drawing. She immediately recognized it, for which he was silently grateful. Then he gave her the card.

She opened it and read:

A Night to Remember

A humid African Christmas Eve
Closed up within a room.
Cigarette smoke eddies under ceiling fans,
And rain beats at the windows dark.

The music is lost in talk;
Tension underlies the laughter.
All eyes see without staring.
At the bar, the two men standing.

"Korea, Vietnam," says one.
"Afghanistan," the other.
The first man steps upon the rail,
A pistol on his ankle shows.

Then through the door she comes,
La plus jolie femme de la chambre.
White gauze she wears, with golden bracelets.
Action freezes, quiet cloaks the room.

She shakes the rain from her golden hair.
Her blue eyes sparkle through the smoke.
She casts a glance around the room
And heads slowly for the bar.

"Scotch, single malt, straight up,"
She tells the Bantu bar m'linzi.
She sips and smiles at all and no one
Then glides off toward the music.

"Korea, Vietnam," says the first.
"That's two to one. We win.
Now I have another thing to do."
The second, "Not so fast my friend,

"Before you sortie forth on your campaign,
I can but only warn you.
I see defeat upon your brow
As clearly as I see the rain."

"Nonsense, for I am Colonel KGB
I have power, wealth, and status.
No woman can I not have
Who knows how we play this great game."

"I see," the second says.
"You may be Colonel KGB
But since first ever I saw her,
She's been the captain of my heart."

He leaves the bar and walks to her,
Their eyes lock, green on blue.
"What are you doing New Year's Eve?
It will be a fine evening for a wedding."

She smiles and takes his arm in hers,
On tiptoe does she rise.
She kisses him on his cheek
And spins into his tight embrace.

He kisses her long upon the lips,
And as they break, aloft he holds two fingers,
As if to say, "That's two to two.
A coup, and now we have a tie."

Four and twenty years on,
She looks across at him.
He smiles, and winks, and casually croons,
"What are we doing New Year's Eve?"

His poetic effort seemed better than his artistic, for with tears in her eyes, she reached for his hand, and pulling it to her cheek, kissed it. Recognizing that something special was happening, the headwaiter applauded, and his applause was taken up by the other waiters and then the habitués who knew the couple. Everyone smiled. Everyone felt good.

He leaned across the table and quietly sang, "What are we doing New Year's Eve?"

THE THIEF

2005, Paris

"IT'S NOT GOING TO BE a problem, and I'll only do it once." He was sweating as he mumbled to himself. "I'll only do it once." It was said as a promise to himself, but it may have been an offer to bargain with God. Truly, it seemed no greater an offense than eating one of the small pies in his mother's refrigerator, the one she'd saved for guests. "Just one," he would say, but he always came back for another. They were just too good. Boy, did he miss that refrigerator. What he could do now with some bologna and bread, a bit of mustard, and some of those little pickles she used to keep in the door. The thought only made his stomach rumble more. He pushed in with his hand, and the rumbling moved into his lower stomach, as if it were inside a long thin balloon being tied by a clown into a giraffe or some other zoo animal.

"It'll be easy," he mumbled once again. "Easy. I've seen it done lots of times. You pick out a woman, follow her, and when the moment is right you grab her purse and run. She's surprised and shouts, 'Stop, thief!' but nobody stops you. You make the nearest corner, take the cash from the purse, and then throw the purse into a waste bin."

"But it has to be the right woman," he thought, "preferably one who doesn't have a strap on her purse or who isn't carrying the strap so that it crosses her chest. A woman in heels is also good because she can't run to chase you, and if she does, she'll fall, and everyone will be helping her up and not chasing you. It'll be easy." He almost hyperventilated as he repeated to himself, "Easy."

So now he had to find the woman—the right woman— and he began to scan the streets.

"But none of this would be necessary if someone would just buy one of my paintings." He just couldn't let go of what he saw as a lack of perception in people today. No one appreciated good art—nice art, solid art. Colorful canvases of picturesque buildings in the city, or landscapes of the parks, or maybe one of his rustic scenes of the outlying farms. If only someone could see the true value in his paintings he would not have to do this. But as things were, he couldn't even trade his paintings for a meal. "They are all Goths, really—Visigoths and Ostrogoths and whatever other kind of Goth doesn't appreciate good art," he mumbled as he scanned the people in the street.

He had tried begging, but his clothes were too nice for anyone to take him seriously. Yes, this was the only way, and besides, no one would suspect him, for what was it they say about crime? The only thing worse than an eyewitness is two eyewitnesses. Yes, he could hear them now.

First eyewitness: "Yes, he was medium height, he wore a white shirt with vertical red stripes and jeans, he had dark hair, and I think he had a mustache." Second eyewitness: "No, he was taller than medium, much taller, and yes the shirt was whitish, more a cream I think, and the stripes were not vertical or red. They were horizontal and black, like a sailor's shirt. His hair was light brown, and I didn't see a mustache."

No, they would never identify him—too many witnesses.

This made him breathe easier. At least he was not still hyperventilating.

But wait—there, on the corner, was the purse. It was the perfect purse. It was long and thin with a fold-over top; there was no strap, and the woman who carried it seemed not worried about its safety as she held it in her hand which she swung forward and backward as she walked. But yes, this was going to be easy.

He crossed the street behind her. She was not too old, maybe as old as he, perhaps a bit younger. She wore a strapless sundress that was a print of yellow, red, and purple flowers on a white background. Her breasts were not too large nor so small that they did not hold up the dress. Like her purse they were perfect, or at least he thought so. She was tan but not that "tanning booth or hanging out too much at the beach" tan. Just the perfect tan that one achieves when one is outside doing things. Her legs were nice and muscular, "She must walk a lot," he whispered to himself. "Or maybe she's a runner."

"That's not good," he thought. A runner might be able to catch up to him if she chased him, but he was reassured since she wore wedges with two-inch heels. "No way she could run in those." Her hair was light brown with highlights from the sun—or maybe a hairdresser—but it hung in ringlets down to her jaw line. He would call it "perky" if he were painting it. He could not see her face as she was walking away from him.

He watched the purse swing back and forth, back and forth. He moved up toward her, preparing to take it on the backswing and run in the direction from which he had come. Three steps more...two...one—she stopped suddenly and turned, the purse gathered up under her arm. She looked across the street. Then she looked directly at him. She looked into his eyes and smiled. He tried to avoid her look but couldn't. He was caught by her green eyes, but then her look turned to one of disappointment. She was looking for someone, and they weren't there. She turned and walked on a few paces. He waited to follow her. Surely he could still have the purse. She would walk on, and the plan would go off just as before, except after only four steps she slid inside the ropes of a street café. She selected an empty table and sat.

He turned and walked back to the edge of a building not fifty feet away. She placed the purse on the table next to her right arm. He had a good view of her. Lightly freckled cheeks with high cheekbones, full but not too full lips colored with the barest of red lipstick, a straight nose that was perfect for her face and those oh-so-green eyes. They were, of course, emerald green, but it was as if the emerald was lit from behind. Her eyes shone green. He wondered how he could capture such a green on the canvas. How does one light a painting from within the canvas?

She waved the waiter away the first time with the dismissive gesture of a trained ballerina. "Yes, she must dance," he thought. "That explains her legs."

The second time the waiter approached he reminded her, "Mademoiselle must order to sit in the enclosure." So she did. "*Campari et soda, s'il vous plait.*" He could hear her voice, not all the words, but the sound of the voice was delightful. Not high or throaty, it sounded like the musical ringing of ice cubes dropping into a fine crystal glass.

She waited, and the purse just lay there on the table for the taking. He could stroll through the enclosure—his clothes would allow him entrance—lift the purse and run toward the next corner. But no, too many chairs and people. He might trip on one of the chair legs and find himself set upon by gallants trying to impress such a beautiful lady. No, he would wait until she left.

She looked impatient when the waiter served her red cocktail. As she drank, the yellow of the lemon-peel garnish highlighted the green of her eyes. Her now stern-looking eyes. He shuddered just a bit in the shadow of the building for he could tell that such eyes could convey anger, and from them might flash a look that could paralyze or even kill, metaphorically speaking. And then, as she lowered the drink, a hand touched her bare shoulder. She smiled.

Her date had arrived. He wore the summer white flannels and sported the too-dark tan of a wastrel. From fifty feet away he could not hide the deepness of the circles under his eyes, caused by too many late nights and too much alcohol. What did she see in this person? Surely those green eyes could discern the deceit in Sir Galahad's brown ones. Those brown eyes laughed and, even from fifty feet, he could tell the laugh of a suitor, for he was sure Brown Eyes was her suitor. But it was a laugh of false bonhomie, a laugh meant to impress, offered up with the necessary head up, leaning backward, and touching of her hand.

This would not do. She was far too fine for this ruffian in a Hermes blazer. The suitor ordered—champagne. "Yes, he would order champagne, wouldn't he?" he thought to himself. "I bet she pays the bill."

He could not hear the remaining conversation for their voices were constrained as they leaned in toward each other. The villain in disguise kept taking her hand, and she kept drawing it back. Perhaps she suspected something. Then the suitor laughed and leaned forward, casually reaching to take up her purse. She grabbed it back from him and standing quickly, opened the purse, drew out some francs, and threw them in his face. She pulled the purse to her chest, as if she was protecting her heart.

"Good! Good!" he thought. "She spotted him for the scoundrel he is. Were I to paint him, it would be with the bumps of his horns showing. It would be the closeted Dorian Gray." He was excited as he watched her spurn the wastrel.

She turned and with quick steps left the enclosure, retreating the way she had entered. She crossed in front of him, but she held the purse tightly. He followed her again across the street where she began to move more slowly. The arm swing was back. She looked over her shoulder toward the café across the street. Was that a smile he saw?

"Yes," he thought, "she knew all along. She knew her suitor was a cad." He was glad for her.

"But I must eat, and I know she has francs in her purse." He moved forward. Again it was three steps, then two—but she rounded a corner, and as he followed, he almost ran her over. She had the purse under her arm as she took a helmet from the storage seat of a Piaggio scooter. Then she turned to him. "Do you mind?" she asked almost coquettishly as she handed him the purse to hold.

"No"—he stumbled in his response—"No, no, not at all."

She pulled the helmet over her head and secured the strap beneath her chin. She pushed the start button, and the Piaggio came to life. Then she reached out with her left hand, *"Merci beaucoup, monsieur."* He handed her the purse as she fixed him with her eyes—her warm, green, laughing eyes. *"Bonjour."*

He watched her fade into the traffic, weaving in and out among the Peugeots and Audis. She was a skilled rider.

And then his stomach reminded him he had not eaten in a day or more.

"Now I have to find another purse," he thought. But—no. He just didn't have the heart to do it. In fact, on reflection he found that he had no heart at all—for the girl with the emerald-green eyes had stolen it.

BETRAYAL

October 9, 197–, article in the Lewistown Montana News

Mummified Remains Found in Cabin Near Little Belt Mountains: Sheriff's deputies found the mummified body of a man in a four-room cabin near the base of the Little Belt Mountains northeast of Judith Gap on Saturday. The deputies were responding to a report of smoke and, fearing another of the arsonist-set grass fires that have plagued the county, arrived quickly. The fire—in what appeared to be a small barn or equipment shed—did not spread, and when deputies searched for the owner of the buildings, they discovered the body. The county coroner was alerted, and the body was removed to the morgue in Great Falls, which is the nearest facility for postmortem examinations. Local residents knew little of the people—they said there had been three—who were staying in the cabin. Most neighbors, the closest being some twelve miles, thought the residents might have been snowbirds who had departed for the winter, although some said they remembered that the cabin seemed occupied last winter.

County records show the cabin is owned by Peter T. Moses of the same address and that he purchased it three years ago. Given the state of the body, the coroner cannot yet say whether foul play may have been involved, but deputies are searching for two people known to have been at least temporary visitors to the cabin, Walter and Laura Meacham, ages about thirty. If readers have any knowledge of the whereabouts of either of these individuals, they should contact the sheriff's department or the Montana State Police.

October 14, 197–, article in the Great Falls, Montana,
newspaper

Coroner Refuses to Say What Killed Judith Gap Mummy.
FBI Called In: *Rodney Smith Reports*: The FBI has taken over the investigation of the mummified remains found stuffed in the chimney of a cabin near the Little Belt Mountains last week. Apparently the body has been moved to a building on Malmstrom Air Force Base outside of town, and an FBI forensics team is coming in from Washington. The local FBI office had no comment on the case when asked by this reporter why they had assumed jurisdiction, but when we took a trip to the cabin, we discovered the entire area has been closed, and there are FBI investigators searching the cabin. Using long-range binoculars, we could see that there were several people in white hazardous material suits coming from the house and the area of the burned barn. Some carried what appeared to be Geiger

counters. Now the question is why. Local authorities and the county coroner's office have all declined to comment on what's happening.

November 01, 197–, Associated Press release

Mystery Mounts on Montana Mummy: Mummified remains found in a remote cabin in Montana have been identified as the body of Peter T. Moses, a former professor of political science who taught at several Ivy League colleges in the 1950s and '60s. Dr. Moses, originally from Boston, held degrees from Harvard College and Cambridge University in England. He was the author of several books describing what he claimed were secret organizations that sought to control the world through manipulation of capital markets. He resigned from his last teaching post two years ago and moved to a cabin near Judith Gap, Montana, to write what he told friends would be the definitive work proving the United States was under the control of a secret cabal of international business interests.

Unnamed sources with access to the FBI claim that searchers at Moses's cabin discovered unexpected levels of a residual radiation although they did not discover any actual radioactive material at the site. Further testing is underway. According to Dr. William Redding of the physics department at the University of Montana, certain radioactive materials have specific fingerprints not unlike some organic materials.

What a professor of political science would be doing with radioactive materials in the middle of Montana is one of the mysteries surrounding this case. Another is the disappearance of Walter and Laura Meacham, who were visiting the professor earlier in the year. They were seen in Lewistown with the professor as late as the middle of March. Attempts to trace the two have been futile. They appear to have arrived in Montana from Canada sometime last year, having listed Lethbridge, Alberta, as their residence on border-crossing cards. They are reported to be driving a maroon 1969 Ford Cortina. People in Lewistown who spoke with them claim both speak English with a touch of a European accent. Walter is described as six feet tall, with dark hair and eyes and a two-inch scar on his cheek just under his right eye. Laura is about five five, with dark shoulder-length hair and brown eyes. There is no indication they have returned to Canada, and Royal Canadian Mounted Police sources claim there is no knowledge of them at the address in Lethbridge they listed as their home.

January 16, 197–, article in the New York Times

Surprise Finding in Montana Case: As if the Watergate mess isn't enough of a problem for the White House, this week unnamed government officials let slip that scientists investigating the radioactive signatures of the residual radiation found in a cabin in Montana last October had confirmed that it matches the signatures for radioactivity contained in some US nuclear missile warheads. Acting FBI Director L. Patrick Gray declined to comment when asked about this during a press conference regarding whether there will be a continued investigation into the Watergate conspiracy. Gray would also not comment on the search for the two Canadians identified in the original Montana investigation.

April 06, 197–, article in the Great Falls newspaper

Air Force Captain Commits Suicide at Malmstrom: The Office of Public Information at Malmstrom AFB confirmed to the news that Captain Thomas M. Massingale, originally of Boston, Massachusetts, committed suicide last Thursday night in his room at the bachelor officers' quarters (BOQ) on base. There was no official report on how the captain took his life, but unofficial sources from the base claim he placed a plastic bag over his head and suffocated himself. The same sources claim his body was found when cleaners entered his room in the BOQ on Friday morning.

According to the press release, Captain Massingale was a team leader for a missile maintenance team assigned to the 341st Strategic Missile Wing at Malmstrom. He had been in the US Air Force for five years, having joined after completing his bachelor's degree in political science at Brown University in Rhode Island. The captain was single, and according to those who knew him, had no girlfriend. He was known for taking long weekends in the surrounding areas and was described as a keen hiker who enjoyed exploring many of the trails in the region. He is said to have been drawing new maps for hiking the trails of the Belt and Little Belt Mountains.

Although investigators did not discover a suicide note they found a poem on Captain Massingale's desk. We have printed a copy for the readers. We should note that written in bold black letters at the bottom of this poem was a phrase that was not part of the poem.

Betrayal

A life long in years occasions profuse tears
Whether outwardly shed or inwardly hid
Loss, failure, pain, the price of gain
But none more than betrayal

The first smites with crushing blow
And wounds grievously both heart and soul
The second less severe and still
The torment great, the wound heals slow.

Then tempered for life, the third and so
Become expected acts to our now wary souls.
Arm's length, tongue quiet, posture more rigid
We arm ourselves 'gainst friend not foe.

But friend is foe, we often find
As time things change within our mind
When love becomes ennui,
And amended is our loyalty.

Not to others do we profess,
But to ourselves we do confess
That it was so all along,
And Master Donne was wrong.

And now as singleton I stand
My shield at the ready, my sword in hand
The hair upon my neck like hackles stout
Warns me of foe and swinging 'bout

I see not foe but friend, dagger raised
But can I strike, or must I stand?
For often have I praised
This friend for his bright deeds.

Still if Europe of a clod be denied
And lessened in its pride,
Then let it be he who pledge forsakes
Not he whose vow a righteous man still makes.

Outwardly will I mourn the death
Of kindred soul departed
While mindfully I seek to know
From where such guile has started.

And finding it will cauterize
All tissue so infected.
For betrayal is an original sin
Birthed by Cain within the glen.

Many tears yet I will weep
And unsound will I sleep
Till another false companion vow breaking
My life or honor does try taking.

But the greatest betrayal is that of untrue love.

Captain Massingale's body has been released to his parents, Dr. Thomas L. and Mrs. Massingale of Amherst, Massachusetts. The funeral will be at the First Congregational Church of Amherst, and burial will be in the church cemetery.

8 September 197–, cablegram from CIA Station Moscow to CIA Headquarters

TOP SECRET: Rumors from sources in Soviet military indicate two GRU (Soviet military intelligence) operatives—a female captain and a male senior lieutenant—received the Red Star for a major foreign intelligence collection effort. NFI (no further information).

9 September 197–, conversation at CIA Headquarters

"Well, that's that. Just as we thought it would be. Has the FBI accepted their failure yet?" This from the CIA director of operations to his chief of counterintelligence as he handed back the manila folder with the Moscow cable.

"No, and I doubt they will. They'll play the 'how on earth could we have known something like this would happen' card. Besides, no one is going to know the details and the Bureau is getting all they can handle from the Watergate thing."

The director sighed. "Still, you know, if we could just get homosexuality into the cultural mainstream, it would solve a lot of our problems with trying to protect secrets."

"Yes, that's true," the counterintelligence chief answered. "Oh, by the way, it was the warhead guidance system they got. I'd sure hate to be the poor SOB in charge of missile security or, for that matter, the special agent in charge of the local FBI office. How much more of this do you think is out there? I mean the thing where the professor is a fellow traveler with the communists and is initially recruited to write books and agitate within the academic community but then is directed to seduce a student who goes on to mine the mother lode of nuclear secrets? But still, something must have gone seriously wrong for them to kill their agent that way; stuffed into a fireplace chimney and smoked. No way, that's just pure mean. So just how many more of these sleeper talent spotters do you think are imbedded in academia searching for the right target to recruit?" The CIA chief is agitated.

"I don't know how many, but certainly more than enough to keep you and me in business; after all, spying, betrayal, envy, anger, revenge, and all the rest of the emotions that espionage embraces and depends on are just basic aspects of human nature. They always have been and always will be. There are just too many peccadilloes of personality and actions that people want to hide from others to ever make it safe to swim in the ocean of secrets that surrounds us."

The Penitent Priest

"Bless me, Father, for I have sinned. It has been five weeks since my last confession…"

And so it went day after day after day. A never-ending succession of idolaters, coveters, adulterers, thieves of things and thoughts, liars, and such. He was a vessel, now over full of the pettiest of sins and emotions. When he was younger, he had thrived on the Christlike emotion of taking others' sins upon himself and absolving the penitents. He suspected they felt relieved when they left the confessional. He wanted them to feel relieved, but he also wanted them to feel renewed in the battle against evil.

"…Go and sin no more." That's what he charged them to do. Go and sin no more. He was sure that many tried. If they weren't trying, they wouldn't come to confession. But he also wondered how many of them used the confessional as an excuse to continue their sinful ways. He had asked his teachers in seminary about this, and he had often spoken of it with his Grace. That is, when the bishop wasn't more concerned about the failing finances of the parish and the dropping enrollment at Saint Benedict's School.

There were people who confessed the same sin over and over. Somehow they felt the absolution they received from him, in some way, made them start fresh from a zero sum position. In truth that was the proposition. They confessed their sins to God through him, and again through him, God absolved them. They were renewed in the faith. Pure as the Paschal Lamb. Still, in his heart, he knew there were those who came to confession seeking the remission of their sins only for the purpose of being able to start with a clean slate. They had no intention of trying not to sin when he charged them. Did that, he asked his monsignor, did that make their absolution null and void? Was their attitude, subconscious as it might be, a sin in itself? And if they were sinning in the confessional and not confessing it, could Jesus actually be the propitiation for their sins? Should he, if he suspected such, withhold absolution? Could he do so purely on suspicion? He struggled with this twice, sometimes three times, a day. On occasion he asked the penitent if he, or she, was omitting a hidden desire to sin again.

Thus had it been the second time the man's voice confessed to forced sex. Something in that voice had tested the priest's resolve. Something pushed him toward the desire to violate the sanctity of the confessional. He strongly cautioned the man to seek assistance. He offered to help the man find that assistance. He instructed that absolution from God did not relieve the man of his duty to obey secular law. The man claimed he was weak. He believed his acts were those of a possession by evil, a possession that set upon him and was too strong for him to resist. But when the priest had suggested exorcism the man refused. He also refused to meet with the priest outside the confessional.

And now the priest heard the voice again through the mesh. "Bless me…"

Again the man claimed possession. That he became a living entity, through whom the devil enjoyed carnal relations. He fought the pleasure. He tried not to enjoy the sex, but he was only human. Evil had once again won out. He fought it. "Oh Father, I fight but I lose. Bless me. Absolve me for being too weak to resist the devil. I promise to resist harder next time."

There it was yet again. "Next time." He knew there would be a "next time" just as the pseudopenitent knew there would be a next time. And no matter how hard he tried, the man would lose the battle to resist, and another woman would be raped. "For it is rape," the priest thought.

He approached the monsignor for guidance, only to hear that which he had been taught in seminary. The sanctity of the confessional is inviolate. It is the very basis of the trust that must exist between the lay and the clergy. The monsignor offered no guidance other than to say the priest should pray for guidance. He also suggested that perhaps the man was just confessing his masturbatory fantasies. Leave it to the monsignor to bring masturbation into the discussion. Whenever their talks involved a troubled teenager, he always managed to hang some of the behavior on problems relating to fantasy and masturbation. He was little help to the priest.

The monsignor, on the other hand, thought he was a great help to the priest but that the priest was becoming "troublesome." That's what he told the bishop. The priest was becoming troublesome. He couldn't let things go and was becoming too embroiled in the troubles he learned about in the confessional. Perhaps it would be best if the bishop moved him. But the priest was doing too good a job at keeping the parish on an even keel in the depth of difficult economic times. No, the bishop could not afford to move the priest, regardless of the monsignor's desire.

While he considered the monsignor's guidance of little value, the priest did consider the possibility of a masturbatory fantasy. Yet he had heard confessions for more than ten years, and he knew fantasy from fact. If it was fantasy, the man still needed help, but the urgency of the affair changed dramatically. He needed to know more about this man. He knew from the voice he was not one of his parishioners. Was there some reason the man had chosen Saint Benedict's? After some thought, he decided to follow the man after his next confession.

First, the priest took to wearing street clothes under his cassock, while leaving his coat in a pew near the side door of the church. But then he remembered how long it takes to unbutton a cassock, so he replaced it with a long surplice over his street clothes. A surplice was quickly drawn over the head on the way to the back of the church.

He waited while absolving petty theft. "Return the item. Make a gift to Saint Jude's and say ten Hail Mary's for strength to resist the urge to own something of someone else's." Impure thoughts: "Concentrate on our Lord's sojourn in Gethsemane where he prayed for strength. Carry your rosary, and when tempted to think impure thoughts, say the rosary to dispel the thoughts." There was covetousness, sloth, and adultery, but no rape.

In the rectory he searched the Internet for local news of rape. There was considerable murder and rape but nothing that seemed to fit what he was hearing from the ersatz penitent. Until, at breakfast one morning, he overheard his housekeeper, Mrs. Malinowski, in an animated discussion with Mrs. O'Shea, his cook.

"It's terrible, I tell you. How many is it now? Five?"

"No, six, they're saying on the morning news. Murder, and all of them strangled. Belt marks around their necks, there were."

"Not just strangled, sodomized too. Men and women they say. Men and women. What kind of devil is out there..." The voices trailed off as they moved back toward the kitchen.

"What kind of devil?" Mrs. O'Shea had asked. What kind of devil, indeed?

The priest had seen the stories on the Internet but had not thought them the work of his rapist. There had been no mention in the confessions of murder, no mention of men. But then there had been no mention of women either. He had simply assumed they had been women.

That afternoon the voice again came clearly through the screen. The priest this time strained to listen for tone. Yes, as he had thought this morning, while the voice sounded a little like that of a weak-willed individual, below the whine there was bravado. If this was a possessed soul, the devil was still there. This was no confession. It was bragging. It was a taunt to the priest, the Church, and to God. It was not enough to exert power over his victims, he must demonstrate his power over God.

The priest asked, "Satan, why do you taunt God?"

"But Father, Satan is no longer in me. I seek absolution. I do not taunt God. I need God's help to resist Satan's power. God has not helped me, but he must. I cannot resist evil on my own. I need your blessing and God's forgiveness. But more than that, I need God to stop the devil."

The priest heard the mocking in the voice. He pondered the moment. He prayed quickly for guidance. "Then my son, go and remember God helps those who help themselves. God will provide you an answer. Go and sin no more."

The man left the confessional and moved quickly down the side aisle toward the main door. The priest furtively parted the curtain at the front of his compartment door to watch the man move off. He saw a man of medium height who walked with the slightest of limps on his right side. His hair was dark; he wore a khaki-colored overcoat. As he reached the door of the church, the priest, who had taken off his surplice in the confessional, sprinted toward the side door, retrieved his jacket from the pew, and quickly donning the jacket, emerged on the side street. He hurried to the main street in time to see the man head toward the subway. It was early for rush hour but the subway was still crowded. The priest had trouble keeping the man in sight, fearing more than once he had lost him. But each time he somehow caught a glimpse and followed him as he left the subway four stops from where he entered. The crush of people on the street grew greater, so the priest walked closer to the man. While he walked he prayed, "Please God, help me. Tell me what I must do." Then they were no longer on a main street, but walking through a series of interconnected alleys.

The man turned right, and the priest lost sight of him. He hurried to make the corner and as he did, he saw that the man stood waiting for him, a thick belt held between his hands. They locked eyes, and the priest stared directly into the eyes of evil. The confessions had not been taunts but challenges. The man spoke, malice resonating in his manner. "Bless me, Father…"

In his next weekly with the monsignor, the priest did not seem so troublesome. He only spoke of his previous problem when directly asked by the monsignor. He replied, "As you suggested, Monsignor, I prayed for guidance, and God answered, just as he answered the penitent's request for help in resisting the devil. But I must confess my earlier doubts that the Church could cope with the man's problems. I also confess that during his last confession I withheld absolution—but I subsequently found the man, and I gave him absolution. I charged him to sin no more, and I'm sure this time he will not."

"You see, Father," the monsignor said. "God provides answers through the Church and his clergy. I hope you will have no other problems of this nature."

The priest, content with himself and the Church, responded, "No, Monsignor, nothing like this issue; but I *am* troubled by a certain serial adulteress in my parish…"

THOMAS WOLFE
WAS RIGHT

August 2003, Zurich

"I wonder what they're doing," he mused. He spun the cylinder on the revolver to check that all ten rounds were firmly settled and then pushed the cylinder into place.

"I bet they've all had lots of kids." He screwed the suppressor onto the barrel of the revolver.

"And they're happy. I hope they're happy. I mean, they deserve to be happy." He checked to ensure his dagger handle was readily accessible in its sheath along the front of his belt.

"I should go back to the reunion and see what's become of them." He dropped an extra magazine into his left field jacket pocket where it joined the 9 mm semiautomatic already there. It was his just-in-case weapon. His "Aw shit!" fall back.

"Yes, that's exactly what I'll do. I'll go back to the reunion." He put the revolver in the deep right-hand pocket of the leather field jacket. He checked to see that all traces of his presence were taken care of and, once again, ensured there were no cuts or tears in the clear latex gloves he wore. Pulling his leather gloves on over the latex, he took up the empty brown-leather briefcase and left the room. He went down the stairs and out into the street.

"I need to take some time off anyway. Besides it's football season back home, and I miss going to the games." He walked the two miles to the building, taking a circuitous route to ensure he was not being followed. He was near the university. He pulled up the hood on the leather field jacket. There were lots of midrise apartment buildings in the area. He entered the entryway of an older, nondescript five-story brick building. He walked up three flights and turned toward an apartment at the back of the landing. Before he knocked he took off his leather gloves, putting them in the empty hand-warmer pockets of his jacket. Then he stood in front of the door's peephole so he could be clearly seen—although the light was such that "clearly" was a relative term. He knocked.

"Min hunak?" (Who's there?) A voice asked in Arabic.

"Abdul Al Haluk," he answered. Abdul the Barber. It was stupid, but that was what they had chosen to call him. Abdul the Barber. The door swung open, right to left. He stepped in to the flat. There were three men at the table. There would be a fourth, the bodyguard, behind the door.

"You have them?" Again the question was in asked in a Saudi dialect.

"Aiwa." (Yes.) He answered in Egyptian. It drove them crazy when he spoke Egyptian to them. He held up the briefcase with its two leather straps buckled firmly in place. He stepped quickly to the table and with a flick of his left wrist lofted the briefcase so it landed in the middle of the tabletop. All three jumped or leaned backward as the briefcase hit the table. The leader leaned back in toward the table to undo the straps of the satchel. As he did so, "Abdul" turned slightly and gestured with his left hand for the man behind the door so he could see the table. As the fourth man moved closer, his attention on the briefcase, he dropped the barrel of the Uzi he held.

At that moment the revolver appeared from the right pocket of the leather field jacket. Generally, one shot to the head with a low velocity .22 hollow point was enough, but he was so quick in his actions he devoted two rounds to the bodyguard. The others received one round each, either in the forehead, or the side of the head nearest the shooter's hand. It took three seconds to fire the five rounds. In that three seconds the leader died in his chair, the man to his left was halfway out of his, and the man to his right was standing, but not yet away from the table.

He checked each of his targets to ensure they were dead. There was time. The apartment was at the back of the building and the suppressor had done its job nicely. He doubted anyone heard the shots. Quickly checking the bodies, he discovered the money they were supposed to pay him for the identity documents and US visas he had promised them. He put it in the briefcase along with the revolver and suppressor, the automatic, extra clip, and killing dagger that he no longer needed. The money wasn't enough to cover the cost of the operation, but every little bit might save the taxpayers something. Still, €25,000 was nothing to sneeze at. Uncounted in the cost equation was the amount saved by taking down four terrorists before they struck. How many taxpayer dollars were saved there? Pulling the hood up over his head again and ensuring the door locked behind him, he headed for his brief exchange with a support operative.

After a mile or so, he was sure he was clean. No one had followed him from the apartment. As he rounded the corner near the baunhaupt, he crossed the street and cut through an alley behind the station that would take him out toward the central park. In a blind area, made by a left followed by a quick right, he passed his contact and the switch was made. He cleared the alley still toting a brown leather briefcase, but this one contained alias-name documents and a train ticket from Zurich to Amsterdam. In Amsterdam another contact would exchange the briefcase for one that contained his true-name documents and an airline ticket from Amsterdam to London. In London he would meet with his handling officer, be debriefed, and then fly to New York. At least, that was his plan.

This was his third operation this year. Amazing how easily you could suck these guys in with the promise of high-quality alias documents, especially excellent US visa impressions. Sometimes all the operation called for was for him to provide the terrorists or other criminals with the documents, and then the FBI tracked them on arrival in the United States. This allowed law enforcement agencies to identify the United States end of the terror or criminal network. But mostly he ended the operation in situ, as he had just done. There would be an anonymous call to the Swiss Surete about a terrorist cell at the apartment, and either the Swiss would take credit, or they would blame the Israelis. It didn't matter. Four more bad guys were dead.

September 2003, London

"How many now?" This from his new debriefing officer.

"That's bad form," he replied.

"Bad form? Why is it bad form?" The young officer was put off.

"Look, do you think I cut notches on the handle of my gun? I don't even own a gun. Maybe you think I take scalps or something? It's a fucking job. It's what I do. I'm good at it. Maybe someday you'll be doing it. I mean, I started right where you are now." He looked at the young inside officer who was tasked to meet with him, go over details of the operation, and provide whatever support was required.

"I thought you'd been doing this forever. Your file doesn't indicate anything about your background. Just that you'd been a deep cover field operative for, well...for a long time." The young officer took a sip of the whiskey he had brought to the meeting.

"I started as an inside officer, just like you. I learned the tricks of the trade from debriefing the old guys before me." He lifted the glass and sniffed. "Jesus, kid, this is Irish whiskey! Jameson! What the hell! Do you think I'm some kind of fucking IRA thug?" He put the glass down. "Irish isn't Scotch! And blended isn't single malt! You missed on both counts. It's forty-three, and if you don't want to be forty-four, you'll fucking well remember Lagavulin, sixteen years, single malt."

"Yes, sir," was both the appropriate, and only, answer the junior officer could muster. "Now, sir, about your next operation."

"No next operation for a while, kiddo. I'm going home."

"Home, sir? Where's home?"

"Never you mind that, Bubba. You don't have a need to know. Tell Langley I need a month's leave. I'll contact them when I head back this way."

He noticed the worried look on the young man's face.

"Hey, just go back and send Langley the message. 'Baldwin from Paladin: Need a month. Going home.' They'll be fine with it."

October 2003, South Texas

The weather was warm and humid. It reminded him of Middle East winters in Jeddah or Abu Dhabi. The hotel ballroom was that cold wet you can only achieve when it's particularly humid outside. South Texas gets that way. It can be eighty-eight degrees on Christmas day and seventeen on New Year's. Depends on when you get a blue norther down from Alberta.

His sun-bleached hair—pretty much gray to begin with—and deep tan didn't make him stand out as much as one might think. He looked not unlike so many in his high school class who were Latinos. His trim appearance, however, did stand out among the spread waistlines that placed buttons under great tension while shirtfronts attempted to constrain stomachs.

The turnout was good. Even after more than thirty years, a majority of the class was still alive. He had little problem recognizing some people, mostly by their voices. Others, though, he didn't have a clue. He had seen none of these people since a visit he made between his junior and senior year in college, and then he had only seen three or four of them. In truth, he was really only interested in speaking with two of these former classmates, both girls—well, of course, women now. One had been his best friend, the other his first great love. Both were on the list of attendees.

He had, as was his practice for functions like this, arrived late, and he would leave early, but even arriving late, he had not seen either of them. The party was well under way. Some seemed to have started their drinking even before the party. He placed himself in a position where he could observe the door to the ballroom and, drink in hand, waited. After ten minutes he saw his friend. She looked a little stouter, but then, svelte had never been her style. Her dark hair, now silver, was still short but not unattractive. He watched her move through the room. Still perky, but not as vivacious as she had been as a teenager. As she closed on him, he noticed her eyes seemed tired. He expected a hug but didn't get one. Her eyes became much colder as she extended her hand.

"And just where in hell have you been for thirty years?" This wasn't the warm welcome he had expected—no, not expected, hoped for. Should he apologize or defend himself? He didn't want a scene, although those in hailing distance had already turned toward them.

"Well, I've been around. You know, here and there. Perhaps not enough here and too much there." That should do.

"Not enough here, how about not here at all? How about no letters, no phone calls? You know, on at least four different occasions I had people tell me you were dead. They told me so often as far as I'm concerned, you are." She turned on a heel and marched off toward the bar. There was a little man in her train he had not noticed earlier. He scooted off after her as a house-slipper–size dog trails his mistress.

Turning back toward the door, he almost spilled his drink against a largish woman who, no doubt, could canoe without need of a life preserver. Her life preservers were encased in a tightly drawn blue sequin dress much too small for the wearer's attributes. Looking down first, to make sure he had not spilled his drink on her dress, he wondered, however, if she did go overboard, would she float head up or head down since her buttocks extended rearward some greater distance than her breasts did forward. Recovering his balance, he began his apology even as his head came up beyond the sweat-glistening mounds of flotation.

"My apologies, Madam…Holy…" He almost said 'crap' but caught himself in time. Please God, no. This could not be her. But, indeed, it was. The dark-haired, blue-eyed, demure young woman of eighteen to whom he had given his heart had become a dyed-platinum oversize harpy, with claws for fingers and a tightness in her face that could only come with staples behind her ears.

"Hey, no problem, Cowboy. Although I'd rather drink that than wear it." Her voice had changed as well. In years long gone, it had always been one of the things he found most appealing about her. There had been the smallest lilt when she spoke. When they were in high school, he could have listened to her all day, but now the voice was hard, demanding. The voice of a woman used to getting what she wanted, and if she didn't, taking people to task for not providing it. He made direct eye contact. She didn't recognize him. "Thank God," he thought.

All these years she had been frozen in his memory as the epitome of womanhood. How many times had he fantasized about the what-ifs of having chosen a different path in life? A path that included his high school sweetheart. Now, all he wondered about was what had become of his letterman's jacket. The one he had given her when they went steady. "Odd," he thought, "now all I want is to get my jacket back after thirty years."

He quickly excused himself. He would try to make up with his friend. He certainly wanted nothing more to do with Mrs. Calabash, or whatever his former sweetheart's now-married name was.

He found his friend at the bar. At least this time she didn't run away.

"Look, Sweet Cheeks," he used the high school nickname she had liked when she was eighteen, but the look she gave him now indicated such intimacy was no longer permitted. "I am sorry. I live a life that keeps me moving around the world. No fixed address for more than a few months at a time."

She looked up into his eyes. Hers were still cold. "Isn't that what American Express offices are for? And what about e-mail? You're not going to tell me you don't have a computer. And then, of course, there's the telephone."

"Well, actually, I don't have a computer. And yes, I suppose I could have written. But can't we let the past be the past?"

She looked at him, her eyes a little softer now. "Yes, we can let the past be the past, but that doesn't mean the future is going to be like the long past that you're thinking about. See the fellow getting me a drink? That's my third fiancé. I can't keep a husband. They all decide to run out on me. Just like you did."

"Hang on a minute," he felt stung by the accusation. "I didn't run out on you. I went off to college in the east, and after college off to the war, and then…well…and then."

She was having none of his explanation. "You know, for somebody so smart, you've never been able to read women, have you? I had the biggest crush on you in high school, but you only had eyes for Ms. Big Tits over there—they're not real you know. There were so many times I wanted to talk to you. So many times I needed your advice, and where were you? Maybe God knew, but I didn't. No, you can't come back into someone's life after thirty years and expect to pick up where you left off."

He was about to plead his case once more when someone slapped him hard on his shoulder. His instinct was to turn, grab the arm and place its owner in a standing arm lock. He resisted, but when he saw who it was, he was sorry he hadn't followed his instincts.

"Hey, look who made it. It's Smart Guy! Hey, Smart Guy, read any good books lately?" It was one of the numerous class bullies who had roamed the halls of the school. Standing beside him was his former henchman, a wannabe bully most people thought of as "Parrot," in that he parroted whatever his leader said.

"Yeah, read any good books lately?" Parrot had not lost his touch.

The two had been large, physically intimidating teenagers in high school. They were still large, but now they were fat as well. Neither of them looked capable of walking a distance greater than recliner to refrigerator without getting winded.

"So tell me, Smart Guy, what do you do for a living? Nobody seems to know."

"Well," he said slowly. "Let me put this into words you'll understand. I'm in the prophylactic business."

"Prophylactics? You mean like—rubbers?" The bully leaned in close, wanting to physically overshadow his correspondent. His breath would have been enough to give away his inebriated state, but he was sweating alcohol as well.

"Something like that. You know, there are prophylactics other than condoms. For example, certain techniques can be used successfully."

"Jesus, you're in the sex business! Hey, everybody"—he raised his voice and swirled his arm above his head, drink in hand—"Smart Guy's in the sex business." He leaned over, leering. "So, can you set me up with some sexy women?"

"I'm not a pimp, and you're drunk. Back off a little. You stink like a gas station men's room."

"What did you just say? You think I smell?"

"No, everybody who has a nose can smell. You stink."

"Why you…" The bully drew back his right hand.

Stepping in close before the bully could swing, he grabbed his opponent's tie, pulled it down with his left hand, and pushed the knot up with his right thumb and forefinger. The knot found the Adam's apple. The bully sputtered, his face became a bright radish red.

He pulled down hard on the tie so the bully's head was level with his own.

"I thought we settled this at the end of our sophomore year." He spoke very slowly into the bully's ear. "How many weeks was it before you didn't have to sit down to pee? How big did they swell up?" He dropped his voice to a whisper. "I have a very sharp knife in my boot, and if you like, I'll be happy to cut them off and make you a nice pouch this time. You can wear them hanging from your belt and show people just how large they are." He released the tie. "Now go and be sick somewhere else." The shove was firm, and the bully staggered backward, struggling to pull his tie loose while gasping for air.

The vanquishing had not been quite as quick as his five-second operation in Zurich earlier that week, but it hadn't taken much longer.

He turned back, looking for his friend, but she had moved on. He scanned the room. His former sweetheart was holding court by the food table. His long-ago friend sat with a group of people at a table in the corner. She was attended by her house-slipper dog of a third fiancé. The bullies had backed as far away as they could, no doubt planning a retribution they would never be courageous enough to carry out.

He shook his head. "Well, I guess I've spent thirty years being in love with the idea of being in love."

As planned, he left early.

November 2003, New York City

He spent two days in New York, revisiting the museums he liked before activating his contact plan. When he did, the message he sent was short: "Baldwin from Paladin. Ready for next assignment. Thomas Wolfe was right. 'You can't go home again.'"

About the Author

TONY JORDAN GREW UP ON the Gulf Coast and graduated with honors from The University of the South in Sewanee, Tennessee. He served as a rescue helicopter pilot in Southeast Asia and later as an instructor, test pilot, and squadron commander in the US Air Force. He became a clandestine operations officer with the Central Intelligence Agency in 1979, where he earned many of that agency's highest awards during a career spanning more than twenty-six years. After several overseas undercover tours as a clandestine operative and five senior leadership positions with the CIA at Langley, he retired, accepting a senior executive position with a major Boston-based research company.

He now writes novels and short stories in the tower office of his cottage on Spy Hill Farm, in the foothills of the Crab Orchard Mountains of Tennessee, where he is ably supported and appropriately encouraged, when needed, by his wife, Anne, and his BFF, Tailwagger Jack.

If you enjoyed this book, please consider posting a written review. Reviews on Amazon and Goodreads are gratefully appreciated. Independent authors depend on word-of-mouth and exposure through sites like these, so anything you can do to help publicize this and other books will help tremendously. Thank you.

77730514R00091

Made in the USA
Columbia, SC
03 October 2017